Baskerville

John
O'CONNELL

Baskerville

**MARBLE ARCH
PRESS**

MARBLE ARCH PRESS

Marble Arch Press
1230 Avenue of the Americas
New York, NY 10020

First Marble Arch Press trade paperback edition June 2013

Marble Arch Press is a publishing collaboration between Short Books, UK and Atria Books, US.

Marble Arch Press and colophon are trademarks of Short Books.

For information about special discounts for bulk purchases, please contact Simon & Schuster Special Sales at 1-866-506-1949 or business@simonandschuster.com

Manufactured in the United States of America

10 9 8 7 6 5 4 3 2 1

ISBN: 978-1-4767-3023-3
ISBN: 978-1-4767-3024-0 (ebook)

For Cathy, Scarlett and Molly

'I really don't know why I have decided to pluck up my courage and present, as if it were authentic, the manuscript of Adso of Melk. Let us say it is an act of love. Or, if you like, a way of ridding myself of numerous, persistent obsessions.'
The Name of the Rose, Umberto Eco

'Art is theft.'
Pablo Picasso

Hôtel Concorde Saint-Lazare
108 Rue Saint-Lazare
Paris
France

WE Crimp, Esq, Solicitor
17 Essex Street
Strand
Westminster
London

December 8th, 1906

Dear Mr Crimp

I am here with Major Matson to see the motor
show and research the 'cursed' mummy case of
Amon-Ra – interviewing curators, archaeologists,
etc who might be able to shed light. We spoke of
this matter when I visited you last month, though I
am not sure how much sense I made.

Doyle has warned me off – you know what he
is like – but I am determined to prove it all nonsense.

On the subject of Doyle, I have written that
account of our dealings over the Baskervilles

business. (I brought it with me to Paris to complete.) I hereby entrust the manuscript to you. The major returns to London tomorrow and offered to deliver it to you in person. I hesitated before accepting as it is an important document. But he is a man of honour.

No-one must read the manuscript until Doyle and I and our immediate descendants are dead. I think a hundred years is about right.

Sincerely,
Your friend
B Fletcher Robinson

Chapter 1

It is often hard to recall the exact circumstances of a meeting. But I can say for certain that I first met Dr Arthur Conan Doyle on the morning of July 11th, 1900. We were waiting to sail from Cape Town back to Southampton on the SS Briton, the most graceful of the Union mail steamers.

Like every other available vessel, the Briton had been requisitioned as a troop transport. It had done well in the early days of the second South African war, rushing out some 1,500 soldiers in under 15 days. Now she was bringing them back; some of them, at any rate, for our fight against the Boer was far from over.

As I leaned over the deck rail, straining for a better view of the gaunt Tommies waiting to board, a voice close behind startled me so that I almost lost my balance.

'Of course,' it said, 'a good many of them will be afflicted by enteric fever.'

It was a deep, confident voice lent charm by a slight Scottish accent. I turned and was confronted by its owner, a man I recognised immediately from engravings and photographs as the creator of Sherlock Holmes; though as I said, I had not met him before.

He, however, believed differently. 'We've been introduced,' he said. 'You are Bertram Fletcher Robinson, journalist and sports writer.'

I agreed that I was. But I also admitted, as I felt I must, that I had no memory of our meeting.

Doyle appeared unconcerned. 'It was at the Reform Club. You are a Reformer, aren't you?'

'I am.'

'Well then,' he said, as if that concluded the matter.

Like me, Doyle is a tall man, his build stout and athletic. But he had lost weight in Bloemfontein, where he was working as voluntary supervisor at Langman's field hospital; so much that his double-breasted linen suit billowed out in a manner it was hard not to find comical.

I had noticed when we shook hands that his skin was clammy. Considering him now, more attentively, it was obvious he was unwell. Every so often a ripple passed across his pale face as if from some palsy. The weather was not yet hot – on the contrary, there a pleasantly light morning breeze – but fat beads of perspiration glistened on his forehead.

Doyle saw my concern. 'Please don't worry,' he

said. 'I was inoculated with the serum on the way out. Whatever this is, it's nothing serious.'

'Can you be sure?'

He smiled weakly. 'Self-diagnosis is a doctor's greatest pleasure.'

We stood there for what might have been ten minutes – not talking, just gazing at what we were shortly to leave behind: Cape Town itself, spread out along the margin of the bay; Table Mountain, whose broad, flattened summit I still longed to visit; and the whole noisy scrum of wharf life, so intoxicating when first you encountered it: Malays and Kaffirs in various states of undress, all wanting to carry your luggage to the custom-house or get you a wagon or sell you fruit – great dewy heaps of purple and white grapes, nectarines, figs, melons, apricots, all wonderfully cheap.

It was Doyle who broke the silence. 'Such a charming place,' he said. 'A fine country. Anyone with any energy could make a fortune here in no time.'

'I've plenty of energy,' I said, 'but not for mining or entrepreneurialism.'

'No? For what, then?'

'I'm to be Managing Editor of the *Daily Express*. It's why I'm returning to London.'

At this Doyle insisted on shaking my hand again. 'My dear fellow, congratulations! They must be pleased with your work out here. Now I remember, there was an *Express* at the hospital and I read one of your dispatches. What was it called – "Cape Town for Empire"? Do I have it right?'

'That was my first,' I pointed out, not without pride.

'Was it? Well, well. It was very good. Very *thoughtful*. I'm writing something myself, as it happens. A history of the conflict. I should have it finished soon.'

He stopped suddenly, gripped the deck rail and shuddered, as if a wave of nausea had overtaken him.

I rushed forward and made to grasp his arm. 'Dr Doyle?'

He put up a hand. 'Please. It will pass. We must talk another time, over dinner. I won't want food tonight, but this thing comes and goes.'

'Perhaps tomorrow evening?'

'Yes, yes. Come to the first-class saloon for seven o'clock.'

With this Doyle turned and, using the rail for support, edged cautiously along the deck in the direction of his cabin.

Doyle had a cabin to himself on the main deck. My quarters were less salubrious, though still not too badly appointed: those of us with War Office press passes were billeted in what would have been first class.

About a hundred soldiers slept on the lower deck in hammocks strung up in rows. I went there only once, in a spirit of journalistic enquiry. I found the conditions cramped and stifling, rendered more unpleasant still by the want of convenience for washing.

Once the anchor was drawn up we soon lost sight of Cape Town and the Cape of Good Hope. Though the sky remained clear and blue, sailing conditions worsened. A heavy beam swell rolled us around and I came close to adding my own weave to the fetid carpet I had noticed on the deck below.

Evidently Doyle felt wretched as well. He postponed our dinner – first one night, then another.

The monotony of shipboard life gets to everyone and I confess I grew jittery and impatient. Weary, too. Too weary to take pleasure in sights I had relished on the way out, like the shoals of flying fish and even the other passing steamers, identification of which had once been the goal of much clamorous and excited sharing of field glasses.

My attempts to organise races and other athletic activities came mostly to nothing. One afternoon I persuaded several soldiers to join me in a game of deck-quoit. When their enthusiasm waned, too quickly for my liking, I passed the time reading and playing chess with a nonconformist missionary whose foul breath I had to turn my head to evade.

I also wrote at length to Gladys, my fiancée, knowing I could post the letter in Las Palmas when we stopped to take on coal.

I told her of my excitement at meeting Doyle. She would understand, I knew; for like me she had read with awe every Sherlock Holmes story. She shared my frustration at Doyle's decision seven years before to kill off the great detective in 'The Final Problem'.

How can I do justice to Gladys?

Perhaps I can't.

Let me just say that while I was away I carried in my head not merely her image – the golden ringlet-ted hair; the light-grey eyes which seem to communicate the finest gradations of thought; the roundness and smoothness of her cheeks – but a sense-memory of her exuberant vitality. It was palpable, physical, like stray hairs left behind on a brush, or the floral smell of her neck as I stooped to kiss her.

Her letters had sustained me on the front line. I loved them for their combination of domestic detail and political analysis; though I confess their naïve radicalism made me smile. Gladys styled herself a 'New Woman', enlightened and alert.

Before I left England she had tried to persuade

me to read a novel, 'The Story of an African Farm', which she assured me would illustrate 'the full complexity of the African predicament'.

I am afraid I put it to one side.

Her letters were full of questions. How was it that a raggle-taggle band of amateur farmers could be a match for the British army? Pax Britannica was all very well, but did we really have a divine right to civilise the world? What if the world chose to resist our interventions?

Still, her most recent letter, dated May 19th, had been full of the celebrations that followed the relief of Mafeking – an event of which everyone has surely heard and which I was fortunate enough to witness at close hand.

In London, so Gladys told me, a large picture of Colonel Baden-Powell had been fixed over the Mansion House balcony. Appearing to huge cheers, the Lord Mayor told the crowd: 'British pluck and valour, when used in a right cause, must triumph.'

Gladys was among the crowd that night. Her friends made sure of it and her letter duly reports it: proof, I think, that for all her convictions she was not immune to pomp.

Four days into the voyage I received word from

Doyle that he was much improved. Would I join him for dinner that evening?

The first-class saloon retained its pre-war air of elegant tranquillity. Doyle arrived ten minutes late, all abustle, apologising for his poor timekeeping. He looked better, sprightlier. His eyes twinkled and his cheeks were ruddy.

'I was distracted by a cockroach in my cabin,' he explained, taking a seat opposite me. 'At first I wasn't sure. I knew it was some species of orthoptera. So I got down on my hands and knees' – he mimed this action – 'and examined it more closely.'

'What did you discover?'

'That its antennae were long and setaceous, while its abdomen had two jointed appendages at the tip. Definitely a cockroach!' Doyle laughed heartily. It was a wonderful sound – rich and warm.

We smoked for some while, then in the dining room had a good meal of beef and potatoes; also the bottle of St Emilion I had won in Ladysmith in a card game and had been keeping for just such an occasion.

Conversation was loose and amiable. It ranged across rugby football – my passion and the subject of a recent book of mine; the difficulty of digging trenches in the dry, rocky soil of the veldt; the rumours that our troops at Mafeking had survived by eating locusts and oat husks. 'If they're true then they shame us all,' said Doyle, and I could only agree.

He was used to boats. As a young man he had gone whaling in the Arctic, then a few years later to West Africa. He had done so to save money to start in practice as a doctor. 'But' – he held up a finger – 'I nearly didn't make it back.'

'No?'

'One afternoon I went swimming at Cape Coast Castle. The black folk jumped into the water freely enough, I didn't see why I shouldn't. It was only later, as I was drying myself on deck...' He paused, smiling.

'What?' I asked. 'What happened?'

'I saw the triangular black fin of a shark rise to the surface!'

You were never sure of the truth of Doyle's stories. That was part of their appeal.

The conditions in the hospital sounded awful. Rows of emaciated men. Flies everywhere – all over your food, forcing themselves into your mouth whenever you tried to eat or speak.

Langman's had erected its tents on a cricket pitch near the centre of Bloemfontein. The pavilion became its main ward. At one end was a stage set for a performance of 'HMS Pinafore'.

Typhoid struck when the Boers cut off the water supply, forcing use of the river and whatever stagnant water could be retrieved from local wells. The stage found itself pushed into service as a latrine – though as Doyle explained, few reached it in time: 'The nurses were busy with their mops!'

There were no coffins. Men were lowered in their blankets into shallow graves at a rate of 60 a day.

It all begged the question: Why had Doyle decided to volunteer? He was a successful author, no longer in youth's impetuous grip; no longer morally obliged to serve his country as he would have been even five years earlier. (He had sought a commission and been rejected as too old: 'At 41! I ask you!') Why, I asked him, had he risked his life and the happiness of his family in this fashion?

He thought for a moment. 'If the health of the Empire is to be honoured, it's a rifle one must grasp, not a wine glass.'

'What about a pen?'

'I grasp that too. But it isn't always enough.'

There was something else, though; another factor in his desire to get away from England and follow an unfamiliar path – caring for his consumptive wife Louisa (or 'Touie', as he called her) had become burdensome.

'I've lived for six years in a sick room,' he said, 'and I'm weary of it.'

He sounded sincere. But I wondered, then as

now, about the extent of his involvement in his wife's care and if his loyalty to her was as profound as he claimed. More than once he mentioned a 'very good friend' by the name of Miss Leckie. Each time, his face flushed and his voice developed a croak so that he had to clear his throat noisily.

It was via this conversational conduit that I was able, eventually, to raise the subject of Sherlock Holmes – one I had avoided as I suspected it was off-limits and did not wish to seem gauche.

Doyle made a reference to this Miss Leckie's skills at plotting, implying that she herself had helped him with some of the stories.

'She goes right to the nub of things,' he said. 'The way she traces the arc of a story, so that irrelevancies fall away. There's something magical about it. Something alchemical, like a burning off of impurities.'

The croak came again. I spied my opening.

'It would be strange,' I began, 'to sit here and not tell you how much I admire your work. "Rodney Stone", for example...'

'Rodney Stone' was a novel about boxing which, as a sportsman, I had enjoyed; though no-one would count it among its author's greatest successes.

Doyle looked pleased. His moustache twitched approvingly.

' "The Tragedy of the Korosko",' I went on. 'It's hard not to think of it, in our current situation. So many scenes imprint themselves on the memory.'

The reader will not need reminding that this novel, one of Doyle's best, unfolds on a River Nile passenger steamer. A group of tourists is attacked and abducted by a band of Dervish warriors.

Doyle raised his hand, bidding this fusillade of praise cease. 'You're very kind,' he said. 'So kind that I hope what I'm about to ask you won't strike you as strange. But I'm curious. Have you read my most recent novel, "A Duet"?'

I admitted I had not and his face fell. 'Its publication coincided with my posting,' I said. 'I couldn't find a copy before I left London.'

Doyle smiled in appreciation of a nice try. 'It didn't catch, that's the truth of it. It was a personal book, and quite effortful – to write, I mean. It's about a marriage. Are you married?'

'I hope to be. I'm engaged.'

'Aha!' He clapped his hands, pleased to lighten the mood. 'Who is she?'

'Gladys Hill Morris. Perhaps you know her father, Philip Richard Morris?'

'Is he a painter?'

'He's known for his maritime scenes.'

'I recognise the name. I don't know his work.'

A silence settled over our table. Doyle drained his glass and looked about him at the other diners. Was he going to call an end to the evening? I couldn't permit that, not yet.

The question burst forth, like a suppressed sneeze: 'And what of Holmes?'

Doyle looked startled. 'Holmes,' he said, as if struggling to recall a figure from the distant past.

'Do you miss him?'

It was an idiotic question. Looking back, I can't believe I asked it.

And yet it was answered.

'I do,' said Doyle, gently. 'It's a curious business, the relationship between a creator and his creations. Brutal, too. One thinks of Gloucester in "King Lear": "As flies to wanton boys are we to the gods,/They kill us for their sport." Of course,' his tone hardened, 'Holmes had to be retired. He was distracting me from better things.'

I seized on this. 'So Holmes is retired? He's not... not *dead*?'

Doyle roared with laughter. 'I like you, Robinson. You remind me of myself when I was younger. But I won't be drawn on that. Goodness, no.'

I woke the next morning at a quarter past five with a pounding headache.

The sea had been rough in the night. Worse, my cabin-mate, Johnny Porter of the *Manchester*

Guardian, snored like an animal. The racket woke me several times. I am not a violent man, but it was all I could do not to shake him awake and yell at him to stop.

We slept fully clothed. This was uncomfortable but made for a simpler waking ritual: shaving in cold water then running 18 times around the deck to improve circulation.

When I arrived at the dining room for breakfast Doyle was already there – frowning at a newspaper, a piece of cutlet grazing his moustache.

I went across to him, nodding at the other diners, some of whom Doyle had introduced me to the previous night: the Duke of Norfolk and his brother Lord Edward Talbot; Lady Sarah Wilson from Mafeking; the Hon Ivor Guest.

Doyle greeted me warmly and motioned for me to sit with him. I ordered a cutlet for myself and a cup of coffee: despite my constitutional I felt groggy and in need of 'pepping up'. Doyle, on the other hand, was bursting with energy. He talked at speed, with a mouth so full it wasn't always easy to understand him.

He said: 'I meant to ask you last night, about the telegraph.'

'Their main man is Bennet Burleigh,' I told him, thinking he meant the newspaper. 'He's a decent chap.'

'No, no,' said Doyle, 'I mean telegraphy itself. Its impact on what you do. Will the outcome of a battle not reach your office by telegraph a day or two before your reports?'

This was a controversial area. Suspicion of the telegraph was widespread among our cadre.

'It's true,' I admitted. 'And if you're asking "Is it harder as a result for us to get scoops?" then the answer is yes. But the war journalist's role is still vital. The telegraph can provide only sketchy details.'

'My dear fellow,' said Doyle, picking up on a defensiveness in my tone, 'I'm not criticising you; merely noting that your role in such a scenario becomes not news-gathering per se but the provision of compelling eyewitness accounts. Tales of derring-do that leap off the page and read as if...' He stopped, a smile forming on his lips.

I frowned. 'As if what?'

'As if you had made them up!'

I felt myself flush; with embarrassment rather than anger, for Doyle had hit the nail on the head. Many such reports — of sieges, battles and conferences — were, I knew well, the invention of people who had been miles away at the time, then forced when finally they arrived on the scene to conjure drama and the illusion of immediacy from whatever was at hand: interviews with participants, survivors' anecdotes, mess-room gossip and a good dose of pure supposition.

The practice was known as 'magic carpeting'. I had indulged in it myself more than once.

'Please, don't take offence. I'm merely observing that the world is changing. Nowadays the job of a correspondent is first and foremost *storytelling*. Tell me, have you ever written fiction?'

'I've tried.'

'What sort?'

'War stories. Detective stories.'

'Give me an example. Of one of your detective plots.'

Now, you will be thinking: How awful, to be put on the spot in such a fashion, and by such a colossus of creative ingenuity!

But I wasn't perturbed. On the contrary, I was confident of impressing Doyle.

Since I first read his Holmes stories as a young man I'd amused myself concocting plots similar to Doyle's, trying to match him twist for twist. You mustn't construe it as boastful if I say I knew the sort of thing he liked.

I had brought with me to Cape Town that famous monograph by Francis Galton on the subject of fingerprints, which championed the use of fingerprinting in forensic science and from which I learnt that the likelihood of two individuals having the same fingerprint is one in 64 billion. The

Fingerprint Bureau at New Scotland Yard would not be created until the following year, but the practice of using fingerprinting to identify and snare criminals had been employed by the Indian police since around 1860.

That it was an intriguing technology was beyond question. But it struck me as open to abuse – blatantly, hideously so. Would it not be simple to create a wax impression of a fingerprint and use it to frame an innocent party by 'stamping' it at a murder scene?

In an idle moment, relaxing on the veldt in a tent belonging to the Bedfordshire Regiment, I had sketched out a plot involving a young lawyer, his mother and an old builder called (I was pleased with this) Jonas Oldacre. The lawyer would discover he was the beneficiary of this Oldacre's will mere hours before the builder was found brutally murdered! The presence of the lawyer's bloody fingerprint on the wall next to the body would satisfy the police, but not my consulting detective, whom I intended to call Addington Peace. (This last detail I chose not to share.)

'What a masterpiece of villainy!' cried Doyle when I had finished. 'And you say this is not a plot you've used yourself?'

'Not yet, no.'

'But you're intending to use it?'

'At some point. When I have the time to do it justice.'

Quick as a flash, Doyle said: 'I'll buy it off you.'

'I'm sorry?'

'I'd like to buy it off you. For £50. Assuming you agree to relinquish all rights of ownership.'

'But that's absurd,' I said.

'No it isn't. It's a wonderful idea and I want to use it. You wouldn't want me to steal it, would you?' He winked at me.

'Of course not.'

'Well then.' He reached into the inside pocket of his jacket, pulled out his wallet and plucked from it a sheaf of notes which he placed on the table before me. 'Take them,' he said, 'before they're mistaken for a tip.'

I picked them up.

'I like the way your mind works,' he said. 'We should work on something together. Pool our resources! What do you say?'

I said I would enjoy that very much.

Before I had a chance to digest what had just happened – England's foremost writer of crime mysteries, a man I had admired from afar for many years, had thought an idea of mine good enough not merely to steal but to pay for, *then suggested we collaborate* – the room hushed as a figure appeared in the doorway.

He was one of the hospital orderlies – a tall, wiry lad of around 18 years. He looked around frantically, then called out: 'Dr Doyle? Is there a Dr Doyle here?'

Doyle raised his hand.

'Please, sir. You must come at once.'

Doyle insisted that I come too. We followed the orderly down onto the troop deck where the hospital was located close to the bows. Inside were seven or eight bunks, all of them occupied. It was dark and intolerably hot – a cheerless place for the sick. My eyes took in the wrecked constitutions of the men before me. Two of them were clearly insane: from sunstroke, I later discovered. They twitched and gibbered, their bloodshot eyes wide with fear.

The hospital sergeant approached us. 'Forgive the intrusion on your journey, Dr Doyle, but our surgeon is bed-bound with fever. And when I heard you were on board...'

'It's no bother,' said Doyle. 'What is the trouble?'

'This man here...' The sergeant led us to the bunk nearest the wall, on which lay the white-faced, glassy-eyed body of a man who in life, to judge by his four chevrons worn points up above the right cuff, had been a regimental sergeant major. His mouth was open, as if he had died shouting at something on the ceiling – some foul succubus waiting to pounce. 'He was admitted yesterday with chest pains,' the sergeant continued. 'This morning he reported some improvement and took a little water. But then, just a few minutes ago, he sat up, thumped his clenched fists against his chest and gave a great roar before falling back onto the mattress.'

Later, Doyle was good enough to tell me exactly what he did in the desperate 15 minutes that followed. For the most part I watched from a distance, knuckle in mouth, almost totally ignorant of the mechanics of the procedure.

Doyle immediately took charge, as one might have expected. His fingers felt for the carotid artery in the man's neck, for the pulse that would have signalled life. But they found nothing.

'He has suffered a cardiac arrest,' said Doyle. 'There is a procedure we might try. I saw it done once by my old teacher in Edinburgh, Dr Joseph Bell.'

He took off his jacket and rolled up his shirt sleeves. An orderly looped an apron over his head. It had once been white; now it was stiff and stinking with blood and pus. When Doyle noticed the state of it he ripped it off and handed it back, saying: 'Don't be a fool, man. Haven't you read Lister?'

Doyle instructed that the man be seated slightly

upright, then undressed so that his chest was exposed. He called for surgical tools and the same orderly handed him a large canvas roll which he spread out before him on the floor. It was lined with pockets for different implements – scalpels; forceps; probes; amputation saws; a trephine; and a wooden, screw-shaped mouth gag.

At this point one of the madmen started bucking in his cot and muttering about the devil having come to fetch him.

I feared he would throw himself off and disturb Doyle, then saw with relief that he was strapped down with a leather belt. At the surgeon's signal, two orderlies went across and sedated him with a hypodermic injection.

Doyle took a clean rag and wiped a solution of phenol across the man's chest before using it to clean his own hands. Its sweet, tarry smell filled the room. Then he took a scalpel and with one smooth sweep made an incision across the breastbone. There was surprisingly little blood.

Next, he gained access to the chest cavity by cutting through the muscle.

'A retractor, please,' he called. 'It's missing from this kit.'

There was no answer. The surgeon and orderlies were too busy staring at the gaping hole in the sergeant major's side.

Doyle grew furious. 'A retractor, damn you! Now! Or I shall report you all!'

They jumped as one at this threat, and after much ransacking of drawers the item was found and slipped into Doyle's now-shaking hand.

Have you ever seen a human heart? I had not, nor have I seen one since that day.

It is a curious thing: so small, somehow, for what it does. And this one was not at its best. I edged forward as Doyle snipped open the pericardium – the sac containing the heart and the roots of the great vessels – and saw his fingers touch the squirming mass; for squirm it did, even though the life had gone from its owner's eyes.

Doyle seemed to read my mind. 'Don't be deceived,' he said. 'It is fibrillating, not beating. There may be nothing I can do. But I must try.'

I saw him take the heart in his hand and squeeze it, not once but many times: firm, rhythmic compressions. It was a difficult job as the organ resisted his grasp, being so wriggly – almost as if a creature were fighting to escape from within – and there being now so much blood around the place.

Minutes passed. The grim tableau remained unchanged. Doyle's actions were having no effect.

Quite suddenly, a noise emanated from deep within the man's open mouth – a sort of hollow, gurgling rasp. It went on and on, and was most distressing to hear.

'Stop. In the name of God, stop!'

I turned, seeking the source of this desperate cry. It was the orderly Doyle had rebuked. He was shaking and had gone quite pale.

'He's dead,' he went on. 'Can't you see that? Leave him be – please!'

I expected Doyle to lose his temper; to ask what right the orderly had to issue orders to a qualified doctor. But he didn't. He paused, as if weighing up what his next course of action should be. Then, very gently, he replaced the heart in the sergeant major's chest and withdrew his bloody hand.

'Perhaps you're right,' he said, straightening himself and turning to face the man. 'Thoracotomy is rarely successful. And he had been gone too long.'

I left that sorry hospital a changed man, one who had been vouchsafed a glimpse behind the too-thin veil that separates the living from the dead.

But something else bothered me.

Thoracotomy is rarely successful.

Doyle had admitted this quite openly. He had implied also that he knew the sergeant major's case to be hopeless from the start.

Why, then, had he attempted the procedure,

which now that it had failed seemed merely messy and invasive?

Was it simply that his taste for theatricality tended towards the morbid? Or had a jaded, middle-aged man, caught between two phases of a life he demanded be packed with activity, tried a little too hard to impress me?

Chapter 2

There are certain situations in life we know will be grave. We expect them, and prepare to be unnerved by them.

Others catch us the opposite way. Their prospect is so exciting that we stride towards them, ready to embrace all they seem to offer us.

Few will be surprised if I say I put the chance to work with Arthur Conan Doyle in the latter category. Though when I look back now, over five years on from the awful events I am about to describe, I wonder if the picture in my head was not already askew; or if there was some symbol – a skull, say, or a chronometer – that I should have noticed and interpreted as a caution.

But I am getting ahead of myself.

First, I must frame my experiences. I must introduce you to my life as it was then in a placid way; let you see me going about my ordinary business, the better to appreciate how extraordinary that life became over the next year.

My most pressing duty once I had returned to England was to travel to Devonshire to visit my parents. The responsibilities of my new job would surely prove too burdensome, certainly in the early months, to permit the taking of days off.

I chose a Tuesday in early August as my date for the trip, reaching Paddington in time to catch the 11.45am fast train to Newton Abbot. The station was furnace-hot, sunlight streaming through the panes of its great roof.

At the book-stall counter, as I was buying a copy of *Punch*, a sharp-eyed little brunette brushed close to me. I thought for a moment that she had picked my pocket. But then I saw her hand over sixpence for one of the cheap editions of Stoker's 'Dracula'.

Smiling, I leaned across and murmured, 'Vampires, indeed.'

She turned and I saw that she was no more than 15. 'Have you read it, sir?'

I said that I had.

'So have I. This is my second copy. I lent the first to a friend and she won't give it back.'

'You like the book, then?'

'Like it?' She narrowed her eyes, as if my question had a hidden meaning. 'It's the most terrifying novel I ever read. The things that happen to poor Lucy… My God, it makes me shudder just to think on them.'

I turned away from her to collect my change and was about to say something more. But when I looked again she had melted into the crowd.

With unusual ease I found a seat in the dining car. I had brought with me several of Doyle's novels, among them 'The White Company' and 'Micah Clarke'. I had read neither, but felt no shame in this. It is hard to keep pace with a writer as prolific as Doyle. He writes for himself, as if to fulfil a physical need: the boundless energy I had witnessed on the Briton had to be channelled somewhere, somehow.

I fell to wondering: had his suggestion that we collaborate been serious? If not, then there was no need for me to slog through 'Micah Clarke'.

As the train began its slow mechanical creep through London's outer suburbs I was more aware than usual – perhaps because I had been in South Africa for so long – of those gradations by which an English city fades into country; the cramped, mean terraces yielding to larger villas and the odd common, then fields and hedgerows: politely tended intimations of the wilderness beyond.

I ate some eggs, then slept for well over an hour.

At Swindon, a waxen-faced clerk seated himself opposite me. He ate his 'grub' with gusto, chuckling all the while over the latest *Tit Bits*. (I longed to ask him which piece he was enjoying so much but feared a long-winded answer.) At Taunton he got out and was replaced by a stout old woman with perfumed hair and the infuriating habit of clicking her tongue against the roof of her mouth.

All the while, Doyle's books remained unread in my hand valise. I simply hadn't the appetite for them.

I let my fingers curl around the small velvet box in my coat pocket. It contained the engagement ring I had brought back from South Africa for Gladys – rose gold, with a large pearl at its centre surrounded by diamonds; quite the most beautiful ring I had ever seen. Terrified of losing the thing, I had resolved to carry it around with me until such time as I could present it to my fiancée.

For yes, as I have mentioned, Gladys and I were already engaged: her father had consented readily. But she had agreed to wait for the ring when I told her that the diamonds available in Cape Town would be far superior – and, though I did not say this, cheaper – than any I might find around Hatton Garden.

'Whatever you think, my dearest,' she said. 'Though you know that the ring could be made of wood for all I care.'

I was glad to see the White Horse as we drew into Westbury. The original is said to have been there for centuries, to have been carved into the hillside to commemorate a victory by King Alfred over the Danes. It has been altered over the years to make it more closely resemble a horse. Indeed, it looked quite different when I was a child, returning with my mother from some excursion to London to buy school uniform or visit Madame Tussaud's. But it never fails to stir patriotic pride in my breast.

Never mind the perils we faced on foreign battlefields, the heart of England was, I felt at that moment, unassailable, the domestic threats from our enemies idle and nebulous: the stuff of fiction.

I took out a pen and notebook and began jotting down possible plots for stories involving my detective Addington Peace.

Perhaps I could persuade Doyle, who was so down on Holmes, to use Peace as his − or rather 'our' − hero instead?

An idea came to me for a murder mystery set during the winter where the weapon was a long icicle, blade-sharp at its tip, which would melt before the body was discovered.

I wrote: 'Icicle too brittle to stab someone with? Check.'

What did Peace look like? I had imagined an aquiline nose; a pursed, unimpressed mouth; thinning hair scraped back.

But perhaps that was too obvious. Perhaps he should be corpulent and foolish, pug-faced, and with a silly foreign accent, so that people were inclined to disregard him and his theories?

It did not matter. Whatever Peace's appearance, the involvement of Doyle would legitimise
him, guaranteeing an audience for subsequent
adventures – adventures I would of course write
myself, for I knew in my heart that Doyle was too
restless to allow himself to be detained beyond an
inaugural outing.

It was still light and warm when I arrived at
Newton Abbot. Baskerville, our family coachman,
was at the station to meet me.

He was only my age but looked ten years older –
his wild hair already grey, his bearing hunched and
abject, as if the demeanour of the faithful retainer
had been bred into his bones. He lived in a cottage
in the grounds of my parents' house at Park Hill,
close to the old drove road.

Baskerville took my bags from the porter and
loaded them onto the coach, an old growler, with
his usual lack of fuss. I sat up next to him, to be
sociable, and on our way out of the town he asked
me about my journey and the situation in South
Africa. His questions were more informed than I
expected and I was pleased to answer them. But
something in his voice told me there was other
business on his mind.

'Come on, Baskerville,' I said. 'Let it out.'

'Well, sir. Not to speak out o' turn, but it's Mr Robinson. He be unwell, I fear. He 'as these pains in 'is chest. Just this mornin' he were took queer.'

This alarmed me. My mother had said nothing of my father's health in any of her letters to me. His condition was a secret, then – one I was duty bound to respect.

My father's name was Joseph. He had retired to Ipplepen in 1882, buying the big house at Park Hill from a bankrupt cider merchant. He worked hard to manoeuvre himself into the heart of the community. He became a magistrate and churchwarden. He joined the Ipplepen Liberal Club, taking a special interest in matters of social welfare.

He had made his fortune as a drug broker – in Liverpool, where I was born. Many of the leading drugs used in this country are the product of other countries and must be imported. Camphor comes from Japan and the East Indies; cassia from the West Indies; hellebore from the mountains of Switzerland and Germany; the best opium from the juice of the Turkish and Egyptian white poppy.

Even in his retirement, my father maintained good relationships with his former suppliers. Gifts of medicines arrived two or three times a year, with the result that his study was a veritable chemist's shop, its shelves stacked with bottles of all shapes and colours, each labelled in his characteristic meticulous script.

He kept the room locked, but I knew where to find the key. When I was sure the household was asleep and there was no-one to hear me creep along the hall, I would let myself in and look up at them in wonderment.

A little later, when I was tall enough, I took the bottles from the shelves and held them up against the oil lamp on his desk, the better to observe the fine powders and viscous fluids and imagine the effects their ingestion might have on me.

How sad it makes me, reviewing the past.

I was twelve when we moved to Ipplepen from Liverpool. Encouraged by my father, I helped the Sexton at our parish church of St Andrew's. I could write and he could not, so after a funeral it became my job to fill in the church ledger.

I remember the entries well.

April 1883: John Swanson buried in new ground, killed by the train from Stoneycombe. 8s 4d.

June 1884: David Cooper was buried from the Asylum aged 71 years. 7s.

One awful day, a day that will stay with me forever, we buried the Sexton's own daughter.

John O'Connell

August 6 1885: Dear little Alice was buried aged 8 and a half. No fees.

She died after an asthma attack. When he heard the news my father was inconsolable. He said, 'But I could have saved her. I have Belladonna here, and Sulphate of Zinc. Barnes knows me and what I did for a living. Why didn't he ask for my help?'

I could not answer him then, but I can now: the man was simply unaware that help was available, that anything could be done to ease his daughter's plight. He lived as so many of his kind live, on the margins of our modern world of science and progress. And you must believe me when I say that is no place to be.

I was 15 when Alice died. But the gap in age did not affect our friendship. I saw a lot of her and grew to love her as a sister, the sister I never had. On her side, I suppose I was a sort of replacement for her brother, Fred, who had left Ipplepen to join the navy.

She lived in a tiny cottage on Fore Street and was always pristine, her clothes clean and pressed, her hair and skin smelling of coal tar soap.

She had a cat, Joseph. When it died she came to me and asked if I would help her dig a grave for it in the churchyard. I said that the graveyard was hallowed ground; you could not bury animals there.

'Why not?' she asked, her breath hot and teary on my face. 'He never hurt anyone. He was the best cat that ever lived.'

'I am sure he was,' I said, 'but animals do not have souls.'

This made her furious. 'How do you know? How can anyone know such a thing?'

I said, 'That is a question for your father.'

'He wouldn't have a view. He is too busy cutting the grass or mending the church roof to think about such things.'

'Are you saying he wouldn't care one way or the other? About where you buried Joseph?'

'I honestly believe it,' she said.

The next day, early in the morning when no-one was around, I met her in the churchyard. We found a space over on the far side, next to the wall. I had brought a trowel and a paper bag to use as a shroud. She brought the cat in a small wooden box. She had scattered wild herbs over its rigid corpse and put little trinkets next to it, little mementoes. She wanted to bury the box but I could not dig deep enough for it to fit, the ground was too hard.

She took this disappointment well.

I worried that the grave we eventually managed to dig was too shallow, that animals would find the body and desecrate it. But that was not really the point. The point was to lay Joseph to rest.

John O'Connell

Afterwards, Alice cried and asked me to hug her. I took her in my arms and let her bury her face in my shoulder as she wept.

I will never forget that moment, nor its grotesque opposite: the moment only months later when I stood over her lifeless body in the vestry, assisting the Sexton and the undertaker in a task no father should ever have to perform.

I begged my father to let me off the laying out, for it was he who had insisted I 'share the benefit of my education with the wider community' by working at the church. But he said I should go: 'It will teach you dispassion – a necessary quality in a doctor.'

'I don't want to be a doctor,' I protested. 'I want to be a writer.'

'Yes, yes,' said my father. 'And I want to fly to the moon.'

At Park Hill I was welcomed with affection and led straight through to the dining room where Mrs Saxham had laid out a simple supper of cold cuts.

I scrutinised my father for signs of illness. His face, I fancied, was a little pale. But otherwise he was full of vigour: loquacious and scholarly, and pleased to be so – as if he had sloughed off the hard skin of the businessman he had once been and found this new untested personality beneath.

Still, he had a businessman's shrewdness. My new job vexed him. Why, he wondered between mouthfuls of tongue, was I so set on working for others? Why not work for myself? It wasn't just a question of money, but of security. 'You're not a young man any longer,' he said. 'You should be looking to the future.'

I tried to explain that this was what freelance writing and editing had involved – working for myself; also that Managing Editor of the *Daily Express* was a good, secure job. But of course, he did not approve of the *Daily Express*. 'Simple stuff for clerks', he called it.

He saw me stiffen and his tone grew more emollient. 'If you're to succeed in London as a writer and editor you need a more central address. Where are you now? Enfield? That won't do at all.'

I admitted it would be helpful to live closer to Fleet Street.

'Your uncle needs someone to live with him,' he said. 'He's all by himself in that great house in Kensington. I'll write to him this evening.'

Do you know my uncle, Sir John Robinson? He was a formidable man, one of the greatest journalists of the age. He had recently retired as Manager and Editor of the *London Daily News*, and the rumour at the Reform, where our paths sometimes crossed, was that he intended to write his memoirs. His villa on Addison Crescent was a vast Georgian affair. The idea of living there appealed to me greatly.

I said as much to my father who promptly finished his plate and went to his study, leaving me alone with my mother. A cloud of foreboding settled about my ears, for I knew the turn the conversation would take.

With a lace handkerchief my mother dabbed at her mouth. She might have been raising a rifle to her shoulder. 'Tell me, Bertie,' she said. 'Tell me about Gladys. Is she well?'

'She's quite well, thank you.'

'We're hoping to meet her soon.'

'That's good,' I said. 'It's my intention to arrange a meeting.'

A shudder, barely perceptible; then the torture continued. 'In your letters – which we found most interesting, thank you – you mentioned that Gladys holds progressive views. How progressive? Is she, for example, a suffragette?'

'She would prefer "suffragist" – "suffragette" is the *Daily Mail*'s belittling coinage. But yes, she believes in the vote for women. And in promoting the cause through peaceful protest.'

'I see.' A pause. 'What did you say her background was?'

'Her father is a painter – Philip Richard Morris.

He's an associate of the Royal Academy and…'

'Yes, yes,' she cut me off, 'I remember. I meant Gladys herself. What did she do? Before you knew her?'

I felt my voice crack as I said, 'I believe she was an actress.'

'An actress. On the stage.'

'Yes.'

'But she no longer acts?'

'No.'

A frown creased her placid brow. 'It's some years since your father and I attended the theatre. Especially the London theatre. But we used to go, now and then, if we were staying with your uncle or my sister.' Her eyes narrowed as she moved in for the kill. 'What might we have seen Gladys in?'

There was only one answer I could give. 'I'm afraid I don't know.'

'You don't? How extraordinary. Perhaps you could ask her?'

'It isn't a period she cares to discuss.'

A burst of horrid laughter. 'I should think not!'

I felt my face redden and my pulse quicken. 'The last time I spoke to father about the suffragists,' I countered, wishing to steer my mother away from the actress question, 'he was sympathetic to their aims. I'm surprised you are not more sympathetic yourself, being a woman.'

John O'Connell

'I have no need for the vote. Women voting would be like men doing needlework.' She looked across at the overmantel, where several Wedgwood pieces stood perfectly spaced. 'I must say, I never thought of you as a bold crusader, or even what I call a natural liberal. Your opinions have always been perfectly commonplace.' She smiled. 'Like my own.'

'I prefer to think of myself as having the common touch,' I said, levelly, willing myself not to lose my temper.

'The common touch!' She gave a little shriek. 'It sounds a horrible affliction. You must ask your father if he has something for it on his shelves.'

My father's sudden entrance saved us. 'The letter is written,' he said. 'I asked John to leave a note for you at the Reform, saying aye or no.' He noticed the sulphurous taste in the air. 'Is everything all right?'

'Quite all right,' I said.

'Good. I thought tomorrow you and I could ride out somewhere. Not far. I can't ride far these days.' His eyes met my mother's and I saw some understanding pass between them.

'I'm afraid I must leave tomorrow morning,' I said. 'I start at the *Express* next week and I have a lot to do before then.'

My father looked genuinely aggrieved. 'I'm sorry

to hear that,' he said.

'So am I,' added my mother. 'Still, you must give Gladys our regards.'

'Yes,' said my father, brightening. 'We're looking forward to meeting her. Perhaps your mother said?'

In truth I could have stayed longer, and would have done had things gone differently. But I could not stand to be in my mother's presence; could not stand to hear Gladys spoken of in that sour, hateful way.

As he took me back to Newton Abbot, Baskerville's disapproval was like a black phantom sitting between us. Evidently, he felt I should have waited to get the measure of my father's ill-health. But I had to tell him that I had seen nothing amiss.

'He'll be 'iding it from you, sir,' he said, at which I snapped and told him not to be so impudent.

Only then did I realise that I had forgotten to mention anything about my meeting with Doyle. By the same token, my parents had failed to raise the topic, even though I had devoted several paragraphs to it in my last letter to them.

Suddenly I was 12 years' old again, full of puerile self-pity and impotent rage. Had they no useful, dare I say intellectual interest in my life? What did I have to do to impress them? What did they want me to be?

Two days later, the promised note from my uncle found its way to me. He was 'delighted' to be in a position to help and hoped I might help him in turn by proof-reading the first few completed chapters of his memoir – to be called 'Fifty Years of Fleet Street'.

I arrived on Uncle John's doorstep amid a litter of packing-boxes. He greeted me with great cheer and led me to my quarters – a pleasant, spacious set on the second floor which reminded me of my rooms at Cambridge.

Uncle John looked nothing like my pinched, wiry father. (He had heard nothing, incidentally, to suggest his brother was in anything but the rudest health.) He had reddish-brown hair, a full beard and a heavy, drooping moustache. Thick-set by nature, he had lost weight recently by living for six months on a diet of lean meat, dry toast and tea without milk or sugar – so much weight that he had had to give away many of his clothes.

In the evening we had a game pie from Fortnum & Mason, brought to us by Nancy, his meek little maid-of-all-work: Mrs Higgins, the cook, was at home with influenza.

Afterwards, in the drawing room, we drank whisky and talked until the flicker of the dying fire lit the pictures and ceiling with a fitful glow. My uncle's company was refreshing after the slog of Ipplepen. Put simply, we understood journalism, therefore we understood each other.

We were not long off turning in when Uncle John said: 'I gather from Doyle that you met on the way back from Cape Town. Tell me, what did you make of him?'

'I liked him a lot,' I said. 'I found him inspiring and amusing.'

'Amusing!' My uncle laughed. 'He certainly is. We've had many a crack at the Reform, Doyle and I. You didn't know I knew him?'

I shook my head.

'He said he only realised later that you and I were related. Did he talk about America?'

'No.'

'Shame. Doyle is interesting on America. Did he talk about Landseer?'

'The painter? He didn't, no. Why?'

'Doyle enjoys Landseer, while I find him an abomination. I ask you, what sort of society revels in pictures of suffering animals?'

I shrugged, for it was not a question I could

easily answer, it never having occurred to me that any society did such a thing.

'You don't mind "The Otter Hunt"? Or "Swannery Invaded By Eagles"?'

'I admire their realism,' I said, carefully. 'I've never given much thought to their... moral content.'

Uncle John frowned. 'I forgot. You are a hunting man, like your father.'

'I ride to hounds, yes.'

'Hunting is an abomination. Tell me, do you enjoy Doyle's books?'

'Very much. That is to say, most of them. "Micah Clarke"... I'm half way through it and, well, it isn't what I expected.'

'Is that the one about what's-it – the Monmouth Rebellion? I didn't read it. It sounded dull. I enjoy Brigadier Gerard, though. He gets the job done. Holmes I found foolish. I'm not being two-faced, by the way – I've said as much to Doyle. I said to him, "I must be the only person in London who gave a cheer when Holmes fell into that waterfall." But he laughed and said, "No, no! I was cheering too!" '

With news instead of advertisements on its front page, the halfpenny *Daily Express* was a revolutionary newspaper. It was the brainchild of Arthur

Pearson; an intended rival to the *Daily Mail*, whose circulation by this time stood at close to a million copies.

News was vital, of course; but so were stories and 'feature' pieces. To quote from my uncle's memoir – appreciatively reviewed when it finally appeared – 'There is no aspect of life now that is not dealt with in our daily papers. They have extended their view farther afield in every direction, and subjects formerly left exclusively to the literary and social reviews or magazines are considered well within their province.'

I think of this passage when I remember my first day as Managing Editor – striding along Fleet Street, past the cab-touts and costermongers, in the heat of a late summer morning.

Pearson's secretary brought me coffee. I drank it in the reception area, my stomach squealing with nerves.

Minutes later, the same secretary accompanied me in the lift to Pearson's suite on the top floor. The journey seemed to take forever. There was much clanking and grinding of gears and pulleys. I was relieved when finally we stopped and the cage jolted open.

We stepped out into what I would later discover was an antechamber or 'holding area': a conventional office, albeit on a grand scale. A row of clocks ticked soothingly on the wall, their hands set variously to show the time in London, New York, Calcutta and Cape Town.

Facing you as you entered was a painting I recognised as the work of John Atkinson Grimshaw. A rain-lashed London street split the moon's reflection into a thousand dancing fragments. The windows of tenement blocks glowed a fiery orange. Silhouetted figures held their umbrellas like pistols, though whether they intended to shoot each other or themselves was not immediately clear.

The painting was half reassuring in its familiarity, half unspeakably bleak.

Pearson was seated behind a large walnut desk, behind which stood a large walnut book case stacked with files and bound documents – perhaps 'back issues' of the paper. Complementing this, in the middle of the room, was a large walnut table with a variety of comfortable-looking chairs and benches arranged around it.

When he saw me Pearson rose and strode across to shake my hand.

'Robinson!' he cried. 'Come and look at this.' He led me across to the table, which was strewn with the proofs of what looked to be a lengthy article by the explorer and adventurer Hesketh Hesketh-Pritchard.

'Hex', as people called him, was one of

Pearson's favourite writers: a demon fast-bowler with a shock of blond hair and the unusual – you must take my word for it – ability to produce exactly what was required of him, be it a ghost story starring his 'psychic detective' Flaxman Low or a travel piece in which action and meditation were happy allies.

Earlier in the year, Hex had gone to Haiti to uncover the secrets of voodoo. Now Pearson had sent him to Patagonia to investigate reports that a giant hairy mammal, believed to be a ground sloth of a type long extinct, was running rampant in its forests. The Mylodon, people called it.

'Tremendous chap, Hex,' said Pearson. 'He'll do anything. You know he takes his mother along with him? She was supposed to go to Haiti. But then she didn't.'

'Why not?'

'I don't know. She got as far as Jamaica then bailed out. Can't say I blame her. Hex nearly died – did you hear? Poison, or something.' A curious faraway look came into his eyes. 'Wait here a tick. I need to point Percy at the porcelain.'

He crossed the room at a great pace and disappeared through a doorway. He left the door ajar so that the splash of fulsome micturition echoed around as I took in Hex's opening paragraph:

'In Patagonia,' I read, 'one stands face to face

with the elemental. As you travel into the interior, Nature, with her large loose grasp, enfolds you. There is no possibility of being mentally propped up by one's fellow man. Empty leagues upon leagues surround you on every side, the inverted bowl we call the sky above.'

I didn't hear Pearson emerge. He crept up behind me, shaking the water from his hands. 'Well? What do you think?'

'It's certainly powerful,' I said.

'It is, isn't it? I feel quite as if I'm there with him.'

'And has he found it yet?'

'What?'

'The Mylodon.'

'God, no. I hope not, anyway. I need to string this out for at least six months just to cover the basic costs. Anyway, look, before you go off to meet your team...'

And he reiterated those pieces of advice he had given me when we met all those months before to discuss my appointment.

The most important of these was: keep the paper unpretentious. Use no foreign words or phrases unless accompanied by a translation, and in general, when writing headlines and leaders, 'never forget the cabman's wife'.

'Oh,' he added, as I was about to take my leave,

'I asked Kipling to write a story for us. He sounded keen. Chase him up, will you?'

I said that I would.

My office sweltered behind glass walls at one end of a vast L-shaped room. Its ambience suggested a medieval hall on a feast day. Some fifty men worked like demons in a fug of pipe smoke and argument.

If I may draw a parallel with rugby-football: Baron Pierre de Coubertin has written that what is admirable in that game is the 'perpetual mix of individualism and discipline, the necessity for one man to think, anticipate, take a decision and at the same time subordinate one's reasoning, thoughts and decisions to those of the captain'.

At the *Express*, I was that captain, and it was a job I relished.

I worked late into the night, correcting proofs and cutting down paragraphs. But it always felt more like play than work. Indeed, I grew to love the printed slips which the sub-editor would lay before me during the course of the day, suggesting new subjects for consideration or reminding me to review the leaders when written.

It helped that we were equipped with all the latest mechanical appliances.

No newspaper could have survived without its telegraph machine – in our case a Wheatstone's ABC, its two circular dials marked with the letters of the alphabet. But we also possessed several telephones and had made great strides with wireless telegraphy: two years before, our sister paper in Dublin had used Marconi's ethereal method to report the results of the Kingston Regatta – the first time this had been attempted.

A year later, Marconi would radiotelegraph the letter S across the Atlantic.

Science annihilates distance, someone once said. All the same, I wonder sometimes whether we would be happier if we were not always craving proximity.

Chapter 3

'Have you heard yet from Doyle?'
          'No.'
'I thought you were going to write a story to-
gether.'
'That was just something he said. To be polite.'
'You must pursue it. Go to the Reform when you
think he'll be there.'
'That would look desperate. And undignified.'
'It would look purposeful and committed.'
'Not everyone responds the way you do to pur-
pose and commitment.'
'Doyle would. He's standing for Parliament, isn't
he?'
I stared at Gladys, at the shadow of childish
naivety as it passed across her face. I said: 'I don't
think he's enjoying the experience. It's already
turned nasty and polling day is months off. His
opponents are calling him a "Jesuit lackey".'
'I forgot he was a Catholic.'
'He isn't. Not a practising one, anyway. But he
was raised in the faith. He schooled at an awful
Jesuit place in Lancashire called Stonyhurst.'

'A cousin of mine went there,' said Gladys. 'The monks were vicious. They hit him so hard with a ferule that his fingers broke.' She sighed. 'I hate religion and all it stands for.'

We had taken the electric tram to Purley and were walking on the chalk hills around Riddlesdown. Skylarks sang in the cloudless sky. Butterflies, including a rare Chalkhill Blue, settled beside us on the meadow gate where we stopped to rest. Swathes of late-summer flowers – oxeye daisies, greater yellow-rattles, man orchids – made a rich carpet of the scrubby turf. It was impossible to view the scene without thinking of Monet and the Impressionists.

I said as much to Gladys. She bit her lip. 'I wish father could paint this,' she said.

For Philip Richard Morris was no longer able to paint. Just this week he had resigned from the Royal Academy. Days characterised by debility and neuralgia yielded to nights so dense with morbid imaginings that sleep became impossible for him. Visitors to the family home in St John's Wood found him chair-bound, weeping softly, his legs covered by a rug. Unable to bear the sight of his own unfinished canvases, he had turned them to face the wall.

Was Gladys punishing herself for her father's decline? It seemed that way. Her natural beauty could not easily be quashed, but since my return from South Africa she had started to dress with a deliberate simplicity that bordered on inelegance. A short, plain jacket covered a grey dress with a single row of kilting. Their quality was good enough – ditto that of her laced boots – but really, it was the attire of a work-girl.

'I can't afford luxury,' she said, 'so why pretend I can?'

That morning I had presented her with the ring. Her gratitude was genuine; she even embraced me. But there was a reserve behind it all, a fear (I guessed) that the ring would bind her not simply to me, which she could bear, but to a cramped and restrictive way of life, which she could not.

A wooden ring would have been a comic token. It would have represented anything we wanted. This one – the one I had brought back from Cape Town, the one she kept twisting nervously around her finger – had the weight of a yoke.

'I want to marry you,' Gladys said to me, as we looked north to where the towers of the Crystal Palace winked in the distance, 'but I don't want a life of dependence. I want freedom, opportunity, education.'

'What about fun?'

'I want that too,' she said, frowning. 'Of course I want that.'

'And children?'

She flushed. 'Perhaps.'

I told her I would not be sacrificed at the altar of her causes, however good and brave they were.

She laughed; then took my hand and said: 'Behold the apathy of the comfortable classes.'

'I'm not apathetic,' I protested, half jokingly. 'I have robust opinions on all sorts of issues.' And I went through them, ticking them off on my fingers. 'Immigration, the National Debt, public drunkenness, overcrowding...'

'Overcrowding! People like you blame everything on overcrowding because you secretly hate the poor.'

'I do not hate the poor.'

'You hate the clerks.'

'I edit a paper aimed at clerks. I write for *Cassell's Saturday Journal*, *Pearson's Weekly*, *Tit Bits*. Who reads them? Clerks, for the most part.'

Gladys changed the subject. She was losing one argument so decided to start another. 'In Africa did you ever journey into the interior to see the native tribes?'

'I'm afraid I was rather busy covering the war,' I said, remembering with a twinge of guilt the evenings spent drinking and playing cards with Churchill.

'I have read that the Zulus communicate using clicks. And that the women pierce themselves.' As she said this, my stomach dipped; it was unusual for a woman to speak of such things. 'In the spring the women perform ceremonies to bring down the rain,' Gladys continued. 'They strip, then put on girdles and grass head-dresses. They go from village well to village well, singing and dancing, cleansing them of mud and impurities. No man is permitted to watch.'

I let out a sigh. 'Magic and superstition are all very well. But you cannot build an Empire with them.'

'Quite so. You use blood and terror. Much more effective.' She took my arm. 'Do you remember that meeting we went to in Whitechapel? The little Russian man in the jerkin?'

I nodded. She had begged me to accompany her, back in the spring, to a dingy hall a hundred yards off the Commercial Road at Whitechapel.

'He horrified you, didn't he?'

'Of course,' I said, thinking what a queer place London is: its foreign colonies, with their own religions and clubs and politics, work their way through life just as if they were in Odessa or Hamburg or Milan. 'He was a revolutionary. A madman.'

'But he needed to be. Don't you see? There is no chance of a new and better world until the old one is utterly destroyed.'

It thrilled me, hearing Gladys talk in this way, even if the sentiment was so overblown as to be nonsensical. She was so poised, so confident. I said, 'The problem is, I am not sure which world I belong in, the new one or the old one.'

She stopped walking and looked up at me, her eyes flashing with intelligence. 'You have a foot in each,' she said. 'That is why I love you.'

And she reached up, put her own lips to mine and kissed me.

There is a sense in which this entire account is a confession. For I have done things which, while shameful, I must reveal in the interests of moral clarity; also because they pertain to the awful events I spoke of earlier. Forgiveness I neither request nor expect. But I hope you will try to understand my actions, and not judge me too harshly.

It behoves me to admit that the trip to Riddlesdown, with its attendant kissing and hand-holding, inflamed my passions – passions Gladys, for all her impatience with standard proprieties, felt unable to indulge.

I must say too that our conversation about Doyle had worried me. With the General Election on the horizon I was busy at the *Express* and had not had time to write for myself, or think about ideas for stories. I was unsure if my imagination was even capable of generating such ideas as I had once had, the sort of ideas Arthur Conan Doyle had thought good enough to buy from me wholesale.

Addington Peace remained aloof and spectral. He still had no physical shape, and without that it was hard to conceive of him moving through a physical world, let alone solving a mystery.

I am trying to explain why, after Gladys and I returned to London and I had dropped her off in St John's Wood – she asked me not to come in, in case it upset her father's routine – I bid the cabbie take me on to Southampton Row, to a chemist I know there.

I bought a half-ounce bottle of laudanum, giving the excuse that I had bad dysentery and was about to take a long train journey.

I took a different hansom to the corner of Warren Street. The night was warm. Men stood outside public houses in their shirtsleeves, slurping from foaming jugs and shouting. Cab-touts hovered in doorways. From an alleyway came the sound of a woman singing the wrong words to 'Ta-ra-ra Boom-de-ay' accompanied by an out-of-tune piano. When she stopped there was a burst of dirty laughter.

Up ahead, a fight broke out between two wailing, stumbling women. They scratched at each other with claw-like hands until someone, a young man of 15 or so, found the courage to pull them apart.

The three of them noted me blankly as I passed. Their eyes were black dots, their faces shrunken and lined like dried fruit.

I walked for five minutes until I reached a shabby row of mean houses. I rapped six times on the door of the one nearest the end and was let in by the landlady.

Neither of us spoke. There was no need. I had been here before.

With its curtains drawn the room was intolerably hot, despite the window being open. Even in the low gaslight it looked wretched. A faded rug covered bare boards. A small looking-glass sat upon a chest of drawers. The smell should have turned my stomach, but it did not.

Against the far wall stood an iron-framed bed. And on this bed, naked, lay 'Franny', a person I had known for two or three years as an unfortunate woman.

I do not know how old Franny was. Older than me, certainly. She was comfortingly plump, her skin the colour of a blanched almond. She looked across at me, half-stupefied. 'Daniel?' she called, weakly. 'Is that you?'

'It's Bertie,' I said. 'Remember your Bertie?'

A smile, like a worn-out reflex. 'Course I do. Couldn't forget you, could I? Come 'ere, Bertie, and lie with me.'

Baskerville

When the act was finished I lay there rigid, hating myself for betraying Gladys, for failing to conquer my baser instincts. What would she say if she knew? Would she even speak to me?

The devil in my ear whispered: *But she doesn't know. She won't know. In any case, you are not yet married.*

What would happen, though, if I married Gladys but found myself unable to stop visiting Franny?

I was a prominent newspaperman. Perhaps one day I would be a public figure. What if I was discovered? Followed here and ambushed? Lines from likely newspaper coverage of our divorce trial ran across my brain like ticker-tape.

The revelations in the Robinson suit are of a most hideous and revolting kind...

The evidence of servants, waiters, brothel-keepers and others has exposed the very lowest sort of dissipation...

I drank some of the laudanum and very soon felt better. My anxieties melted away and a glorious insulating numbness suffused me, starting in my head and extending gradually until the whole of my body felt at rest.

Suddenly, somewhere inside my head, a dam burst – and it was as if I had been granted access to a hitherto closed-off wing of my brain. As a journalist, I had never had any difficulty converting the world into words. I did it well enough, I knew. But I had never been able to make those words *glow*;

never had any confidence that anything I wrote might outlast me, or indeed of the measures I would need to take for that to happen. This failure had been a constant source of frustration to me, despite the assurances of commonsensical friends that only a fool tries to annexe posterity.

All of that was changing. As I lay on the bed, Franny lolling next to me, I saw how it could be done so that my desire and my will turned like a wheel, all at one speed.

Sounds came, as if on a gust of wind, as if from the other side of the wall. The clink-clink of pick-axes against rock. The hiss of steam, the grinding of turbines.

The heat grew ever more intense. Above me: a white hole in the sky. It burned into my face so that hot tears of sweat ran down my cheeks. Beneath it, almost close enough to touch, I saw a cross-hatching of aerial ropeways, like a spider's web.

I looked around. I was one of hundreds – hundreds of men, kneeling before fenced-off patches of ground, patches we were striking at again and again with pickaxes. We were at the centre of a vast and craggy crater. Around its rim, huts of corrugated iron stood at regular intervals on sandbagged platforms.

My hands were filthy, covered in scabs and sores. Flies settled on them, feasting on the ooze, not minding the incessant motion, the incessant clink-clink-clink.

Through my pain and exhaustion I felt strongly that whatever this was − a waking dream? An instance of corporeal transfer? − it was intensely true and important; also that these sounds and images were flowing into me in even bursts, as electricity pulses like a heartbeat along a length of cable.

Across to my left, several Kaffirs in loin cloths stood around a great mound of gravel. It glittered as the sun's rays struck it, and I saw that they were sorting through the stones. One would shovel a heap of them into a wooden box. Another would agitate this box with his hands while his companion poured water into it.

The gravel mound was located close to the edge of the mine, at the foot of a precipice, next to a small wooden hut. I had only just noticed this when I noticed something else, something behind it: a scintilla of movement.

The rock face was starting to crumble.

How can I convey the speed of it? Before I had the chance to call out, my ears were filled with the din of crashing timber, my eyes and mouth with dust. Reflexively, I ducked down, put my arms over my head, and waited.

Silence filled the air; but this was like no silence I had experienced. It was a hideous, dissonant caricature, as if the world had lost its capacity for harmony and would never recover it.

When the dust had cleared a number of us rushed across to where the men had been standing only seconds before. Someone called out 'Careful! There might be more!', but we ignored him in our desperation to shift the boulders.

I knew – we all knew – that there was no hope. No-one could possibly survive such an avalanche. Even so, it was a shock when I saw the arm.

It protruded from beneath the rock like a strange and alien flower: the crusted white palm of a black hand. And at its centre was a pitiful thwarted scattering of gravel, stuck to the skin with blood.

I screamed. Then I kept on screaming.

The vision faded. I was back in the dingy bedroom, lying on my back, unable to move a limb.

I had stopped screaming. But it was too late.

Springs squeaked as Franny rose from the bed. She wrapped herself in a shawl and walked across the room without looking at me.

She opened the door and called out, 'Need some 'elp in 'ere, Betty. Gentleman's 'ad a funny turn.'

The heavy thud of boots up the stairs. The doorway filled, first by one man, then another – the largest men I had ever seen, and I am no midget. Two pairs of thick, burly arms dressed me roughly, then scooped me up. One man took my shoulders, the other my feet. They carried me down the stairs like a corpse.

I was heavier than they expected, for I heard one say to the other: 'Big old bastard, innee?'

Came the reply: 'Too right.'

The landlady held open the front door as they threw me out onto the pavement.

It was October when finally I heard from Doyle again. I received in the post a personally inscribed copy of his new book 'The Great Boer War' together with a friendly note asking if I had had any thoughts about 'our great collaboration'.

I was thrilled. No, jubilant. Doyle had been true to his word, and a gentleman cannot be more than that.

I told Gladys and she squealed with delight. 'I am so proud of you, Bertie. Now you must prove that you are a match for him.'

'I'll settle for being his foil,' I said.

She looked at me. 'Will you?'

I replied, thanking him for the book. I told him I had found much to admire in it, though out of a desire not to appear sycophantic I took careful, constructive issue with several of its finer points. I also commiserated over his recent defeat as

John O'Connell

Conservative and Liberal Unionist candidate for Edinburgh Central.

A few days later, Doyle's reply came by telegram.

It said simply: 'How about a spot of golf?'

Chapter 4

It was a grey, cheerless day – a Sunday, as I recall. Doyle and I walked out a hole or two to put a few hillocks between ourselves and the clubhouse. But no sooner had we teed our first balls than the wind whipped itself up, coming in low and cold off the sea, cutting through our tweed coats and knickerbockers.

I felt sorry for my caddy. A short, red-haired boy, he was quite insufficiently clad in a cape better suited to repelling rain than wind. He kept sniffing and wiping his nose with the back of his hand. I passed him a handkerchief, telling him to keep it, and after using it he stuffed it gratefully into his trousers as if I had offered him a wad of notes.

One is dreadfully exposed on Cromer's clifftops, all too aware of the destructive power of the elements.

Three hundred years ago, the sea swallowed an entire village a little way along the coast. Shipden, it was called. Rock lying a quarter of a mile from the shore is said to be the old steeple of its parish church. When the wind is in the right direction, locals believe they can still hear the tolling of its barnacled bells warning them of bad weather.

I had listened out last night but heard no bells; only the wind as it howled around the chimneys and gables of our retreat: the Royal Links Hotel – austere but majestic; like an Austrian castle, if Austrian castles had wrought-iron observation platforms along the side.

Doyle pronounced this last feature 'excellent for birdwatching'. He had risen early this morning and, with his new field glasses, spotted a nesting ringed plover.

On the links, however, his success was less marked. He tapped the ball with his driving-putter, groaning as it veered wildly across the turf.

I saw the problem at once. 'You hit it too hard. A putt *with* the wind requires only a gentle tap compared with a similar putt *against* the wind.'

'I realise that,' he said. 'But a big man fares worse at golf on a windy day. The wind gets hold of our shoulders and interferes with our swing.'

We tried every trick to combat the weather. Teeing the ball down an extra quarter-inch; adjusting our irons; widening our stances. None of it worked. The game was a disaster and demanded to be written off.

As we trudged back from the clubhouse, Doyle said: 'It may be fashionable, but I must confess I am not at all sure about golf.'

'Nor me,' I said. 'I'm a rugby man, pure and simple. While you are, what – a cricket man?'

'Exactly so.' He laughed and slapped me heartily on the back. 'Let this be a lesson to us, Robinson – that men should play to their strengths in life.'

Cromer is charming, I suppose, with its great church and narrow streets. Doyle and I found it charming at any rate, back in April of 1901, some six months after I received his telegram.

April had proved the earliest either of us could get away. We were busy men, our diaries clogged. But Doyle thought this delay to our advantage.

'April is the perfect time to see Cromer,' he said. 'The weather will be fair and it won't be crowded.'

In high season, he explained, the excursion steamers brought hordes of daytrippers across from Yarmouth. They filled the beaches, attracting all manner of parasites – fortune-teller gypsies; stallholders selling bruised fruit and stale gingerbread.

He had stayed in Cromer – and at the Royal Links – before. The hotel stood within the grounds of the Royal Cromer Golf Club where we had attempted to play. It was an 18-hole course on the breezy uplands of the town's Lighthouse Hills. With our new king as its patron, it had become what it remains as I write these words, one of the most popular courses on England's east coast.

It was Henry Irving who commended the hotel to Doyle. The great actor had appeared there in a fundraising gala for the local cottage hospital. Doyle subsequently took Louisa, whose delicate lungs were much helped by the dry, strong air. Now he hoped it might invigorate him in the same way, for he was not a well man: since our return from Cape Town he had grown pale and drawn, with distinct traces of grey in his moustache.

It was not hard to work out why. The hustings will drain life from the sturdiest character; in addition to which Doyle had suffered a relapse of enteric fever; and, like everyone, been badly shaken by the death of Queen Victoria at the start of the year: 'She was the centre of all things. What on earth will happen now?'

There was Jean too, of course.

Being the man he is, Doyle downplayed his loss of agility. 'In golf, mental condition is more important than physical fitness,' he told me. 'You cannot play golf if you are worried in mind.'

He seemed happier back at the hotel, snug in our private sitting room, with hot coffee on the table and the day's papers spread out before us.

A cosy scene, to be sure. And yet I could not relax.

Since our arrival in Cromer the day before I had tried several times to raise the subject of our collaboration, only for Doyle to knock me back with a 'Yes, yes' or start up a fresh conversation about something entirely different.

This made me nervous, for I am at heart a pragmatist. I understood perfectly that for Doyle, while collaboration might be an intriguing diversion from his normal writing practice, it was at the same time inessential, supererogatory. If it happened, then it happened. If not, well, this − the hotel, the view, chatting about sport and the war over half-decent food − was a perfectly pleasant way to pass the time.

There was another matter, too. Doyle had recently given an interview to *Tit Bits* declaring that, although he had 'never for an instant regretted the course I took in killing Sherlock', it did not follow that because the detective was dead he should not write about him again if he wanted to, 'for there is no limit to the number of papers he left behind'.

This seemed an amplification of his comment to me that Holmes had merely been 'retired'. And I could not help wondering if I had played some part in rekindling the Holmesian flame in his jaded imagination.

How ironic, if so. For it was not what I wished for. And it was certainly not what Addington Peace wished for.

There was a rustling sound as Doyle's newspaper fell out of his hands and onto the floor. He was fast asleep.

On a low table in the corner of the room was a small, neat pile of *Strand* magazines. I went over and picked up the issue on the top of the pile. It was the December 1900 issue which, although I take the *Strand*, I had for some reason not seen.

I flicked through the pages and quite by chance came upon 'Followed' by the Irish detective story writer Mrs LT Meade (assisted by Robert Eustace), which I began to read.

Readers familiar with the tale had better skip the following paragraph.

Readers unfamiliar with it who do not wish to read it themselves should know that it concerns a young woman called Flower Dalrymple who is staying at a crumbling manor house on Salisbury Plain. Enraged by Flower's ambitions to marry her son, Flower's soon-to-be mother-in-law, Lady Sarah, tries to kill Flower by sending after her a venomous Tasmanian snake whose bite causes death in six seconds. The snake knows to go after Flower because Lady Sarah has covered one of Flower's brown boots in a snake-attracting powder.

Flower narrates the tale with some gusto, and the climax is quite something. Fortunately the creature is shot and killed just before it reaches Stonehenge. The *Strand*'s illustrator Sidney Paget, who did so much to bring Holmes to life, had produced a marvellous picture.

'You should read this,' I said to my snoozing companion when I had finished it. 'It's rather amusing.'

'What? Eh?' Doyle's eyes opened a crack.

'This story in December's *Strand*. "Followed", by a Mrs LT Meade.'

'Is that the one about the snake?'

'The very same.'

Doyle smiled, then quoted in his most stentorian voice: ' "Every fibre in my body was tingling with terror, for gliding towards me, in great curves, with head raised, was an enormous black snake!" '

I sat up, astonished. 'How did you do that?'

'There's no mystery,' he said. 'I simply remembered it. It's a memorable passage, you must admit. I did wonder if perhaps its author had been influenced by my "Speckled Band". But she insists not.'

'You know her?'

'Oh yes. She's a very pleasant Irish woman called Elizabeth Smith. Robert Eustace is also a *nom de plume*. Actually, I prefer his real name, Robert Barton. It has more gravitas.'

John O'Connell

Later, I grew used to being asked by people who knew of my involvement in what became 'The Hound of the Baskervilles', 'Where did the idea come from?'

This is rarely an easy question for an author to answer. But I can say with certainty that the seed planted itself in our brains the very next moment, the moment our waiter arrived with the plate of crumpets Doyle had ordered.

I cannot speak for Doyle, but the soil of my imagination had been enriched by Meade's story. Crude and sensational though it was, it represented a route-map, a blueprint – call it what you will.

(Much rot is talked about 'inspiration'. In my experience, imagination works primarily by imitating and recombining. The 'creative process' is a matter of compounds interacting with each other – a species of the chemical process Goethe calls elective affinity.)

Doyle was excellent at small talk. He was famous, and as a result people were often tongue-tied around him. On several occasions I watched transfixed as he put admirers at ease by chatting to them about their jobs, the weather, the price of fish.

This was no mere device. He was interested in what they had to say, and as a result what they had to say frequently found its way into his stories.

Into this category I would put our waiter; the cheerful, curly-haired waiter who happened to walk through the door just as Doyle had asked me what I thought about the name Robert Eustace and I was framing my reply.

When he had finished serving us, the waiter asked if he could get us anything else.

Doyle said no, we had everything we desired, thank you. He continued: 'You must think us very lazy. You probably think we should be exploring the chancel ruins, or watching the fishermen mend their nets.'

The waiter laughed. 'Not at all, sir. Just as long as you're not expecting the fishermen to accompany you to the chancel ruins.'

'Why?' I wondered. 'What would be wrong with that?'

'They're scared out of their wits by them. Not by the ruins as such. But by the child.'

'What child?' we both asked.

The waiter looked down and cleared his throat, embarrassed to be sharing silly local gossip with such eminent guests. 'It's said that as you cross the chancel at night, a little child-like figure dressed in white rises from the ground. It increases in height until it is level with you. Then all of a sudden a great gash appears across its throat and blood pours down in a torrent over its white clothes.'

'My God,' said Doyle, softly. 'What happens then?'

'It vanishes like a flash, sir. Leaving a terrible sighing sound in your ears.'

Doyle's manner became urgent and attentive. 'And have you seen this… apparition?'

'No, sir.'

'Has anyone you know seen it?'

'Only Henry King. But he's an old slusspot.'

'A what?'

'Sorry, sir.' The waiter reddened. 'I meant that he likes a drink.'

'No need to apologise,' said Doyle. 'Tell me, is this area known for its ghosts?'

'Oh yes, sir. Out Runton way, people say they've seen a walking light. There was digging a few years back and some bones were disturbed. An urn was destroyed, and some other valuables. The labourer responsible, he's so conscience-stricken, he won't point out the spot where it happened lest a worse thing befall him.' The waiter paused. 'Then of course, there's Black Shuck.'

Doyle frowned. 'I've heard that name before.'

'He's a dog, sir. A devilish, solitary hound – black and shaggy, about the size of a small calf. He goes up and down the coast of Norfolk and Suffolk. But you can't hear him: his tread makes no noise. Cromer is his home, some say. He wanders up from the beach past this very hotel – along the Mill Road, up the hill, then down into the grounds of Cromer Hall. There's a yew valley runs behind it. Black Shuck likes it there.'

'He sounds harmless enough,' said Doyle.

'Oh no, sir.' The waiter's voice cracked and he shook his head so quickly it was like a shudder. 'He's a terrible beast. His eyes glow like coals in the night. You never want to see those eyes, sir. And you never want to be seen by them. For anyone Black Shuck looks at will die within the year.'

I listened, entranced. But of course I knew this story well, or at least a version of it.

On Dartmoor, where I spent so much of my childhood, we have the Whisht Hounds – the devil's own dogs, who prowl over the moor on winter nights in search of the souls of unbaptised babies.

We have Wistman's Wood, a remote copse near Two Bridges, where their Wild Hunt starts.

We have the legend of Richard Cabell, the old squire of Brook near Buckfastleigh, to pass on to our children, and our children's children.

Cabell was an evil man, cruel and abusive, and when he died on July 5th 1677 he was interned in the family tomb at Buckfastleigh Church. So frightened were the parishioners of him escaping that they put a huge stone slab across the top. That night, a pack of phantom hounds came tearing across the moor to sit beside his tomb, and from then on, every year on the anniversary of his death, their ungodly howling echoes around the moor.

Some say Cabell killed his wife in a fit of temper, believing her to have been unfaithful. She had tried to run away from him, up onto the moor. But he caught up with her, and stabbed her.

Fortunately, her faithful hound was by her side. When he saw what had happened, he flew at Cabell and tore out his throat.

When the waiter had left the room (gratefully, bearing an autographed receipt), I told Doyle all of this. As I reached the part about the stone slab he put his hand to his mouth and muttered, 'How absolutely fiendish.'

'Of course,' he said afterwards, 'Dartmoor is extraordinarily rich in folklore.'

(Doyle thought he knew Dartmoor well because he had lived in Plymouth for a time after graduating from Edinburgh University. But he didn't, not really. Think of 'Silver Blaze', where he puts Tavistock 'in the middle of the huge circle of Dartmoor' when it isn't on the moor at all.)

'The stories are preposterous,' I said, 'but compelling all the same.'

Doyle tilted his head. ' "Preposterous" is harsh.'

'I don't mean they aren't valuable as stories.

Legends bind us all together. But if you are asking, "Do Whisht Hounds exist?" – well, I would have to say no.'

Doyle's face became impassive. He was disappointed in me and my hulking insolence. 'Remember your "Hamlet",' he said. '"There are more things in Heaven and Earth, Horatio…"'

'I know. And I understand. But really, Doyle – Whisht Hounds?'

Perhaps he thought I was mocking him. He became huffish and pompous, as if I were a paying crowd at a lecture theatre. 'Humanity will soon be startled,' he declared, 'by some astounding manifestations in connection with the occult sciences. I am not at liberty to indicate what form they will take. But they will have considerable influence on modern thought.'

An embarrassed silence filled the room, punctured only by the fire's crackle and the too-loud ticking of a grandfather clock.

'I am sure you are right,' I said, finally, not wishing to fall out with him over something so foolish. 'There is much that we don't know. About the supernatural.'

He shifted forward in his chair, so that he was able to drum on the table for emphasis. 'The thing you have to ask yourself, Robinson, is this: if it isn't true on some level, *why is it so frightening?* Which brings us to our collaboration…'

My heart leapt to hear the word; and again when he said: 'I think we have found our subject.'

'Ghosts?' I asked, genuinely curious.

'Hounds. Phantom hounds. What do you think?'

I said it was a highly promising idea.

'It will be a creeper,' said Doyle, clapping his hands. 'A real creeper! We will show Bram how it's done. Did you read his "Dracula"?'

'I did,' I said, remembering the sharp-eyed girl at Paddington. Where was she now? What was she reading?

'A great idea, indifferently executed. Too much travelogue. Travelogue wears the reader out.' A second's pause. 'What shall we call it?'

'I don't know,' I said. ' "The Hounds of…" something. I say, shouldn't we decide on a title later? When we know what the story is about?'

'We know what the story is about,' said Doyle, as if to a child. 'It's about some hounds.'

'Right,' I said. 'Of course. Only I thought…'

'What's a good old-fashioned Dartmoor name?'

'We're setting it on Dartmoor?'

'Dartmoor is perfect − the low mist, the bleak terrain.'

'What about here?'

'At the Royal Links?'

'Not the hotel necessarily. But Cromer. We could set it in Cromer. Then the hound could be Black Shuck himself.'

Doyle shut his eyes while he processed this suggestion. 'No,' he said, opening them. 'Cromer isn't mysterious enough. It's too... ordinary.'

Quite suddenly, Hesketh Hesketh-Pritchard's article about Patagonia popped unbidden into my mind. It was the strangest thing, but I found myself able to quote the passage I had read in Pearson's office with the same reflexive ease that Doyle had quoted from 'Followed'.

'In Dartmoor,' I began, 'one stands face to face with the elemental. As you travel into the interior, Nature, with her large loose grasp, enfolds you. There is no possibility of being mentally propped up by one's fellow man. Empty leagues upon leagues surround you on every side, the inverted bowl we call the sky above.'

As I spoke I watched Doyle studying me. I could tell my apparent fluency was puzzling him. Still, he clapped at the end. 'Exactly,' he said, grinning. 'That sums it up so very well. We must put all of that in the story. Really, you have an admirable turn of phrase.'

I made a gesture as if to say, 'It was nothing.' But I was thrilled, obviously; part of the thrill deriving from having got away with something illicit.

There was greater glory to come. As if the word had just come to me, I said quite suddenly: 'Baskerville.'

'I beg your pardon?'

'You wanted a good old-fashioned Dartmoor name. And I thought just now: Baskerville. There are scores of them on Dartmoor. Our family coachman is a Baskerville.' A current of pure joy passed between us as I tried out the title: ' "The Hounds of the Baskervilles".'

'Yes!' Doyle rose suddenly and began to pace the room. 'Yes, yes, yes! Although,' he jabbed at the air, 'the singular would sound better. "The Hound of the Baskervilles". Don't you agree?'

I said that I did agree.

I said that it sounded perfect.

The next day would have been Monday, April 29th, 1901.

It was early afternoon. Although Pearson was at a meeting, his secretary let me sit alone in his office while I awaited his return. I was now a known quantity, a trusted party, the successful editor of a successful national newspaper: unlikely, on balance, to scratch my initials into the furniture or walk off with confidential papers.

I can see now that the Grimshaw painting on Pearson's wall was warning me, had been warning me all along. *Be careful, Robinson. Stay close to what you know, and to the people you love.* Those commuters trudging home in the dark with their umbrellas – they were my true concern. I livened up their breakfasts and train journeys, and in return they paid my wages. I had more, much more, in common with them than with Arthur Conan Doyle.

But I could think about nothing save the 'Baskervilles' project. The preoccupation was intense, almost violent, like a bunched fist buried in my chest. Even in the earliest days of my relationship with Gladys I had experienced nothing like this. But of course, love and vanity are closely aligned.

I stood up to greet Pearson. He was tense and harried, not his usual jovial self.

'So you want time off,' he said, hanging up his coat and hat. 'Time off is fine. We all need time off. But this is damned short notice.'

'I'm sorry,' I said. 'It is rather an extraordinary situation.'

'It's the talk of London, that's what it is. I've just come from the Reform. Your uncle's been telling everyone.'

'I asked him to keep it to himself.'

'Did you? That was hopeful. You might as well ask our future king to stop whoring.' He sighed and rubbed his bloodshot eyes. '"Edward VII". Honestly. I shall never get used to it.'

I had returned to Kensington the previous night to find my uncle standing in the hallway before a painting of some dogs.

He was weeping openly – not because the dogs were suffering, but because they were happy.

'Oh, Bertie, it's you. Come over here. I bought this today from a little gallery in Bloomsbury. The brushwork is quite exquisite.'

I went over and stood by him. The painting was grotesque in every way. There were three labrador puppies in a basket. One was licking its neighbour; another batted with its paw at a butterfly that had dared to come too close.

'Look,' said Uncle John, pointing. 'Look at their little noses.'

I muttered something to the effect that it was delightful, then got to the point: 'May I dine with you tonight, uncle? There's something I'd like to discuss.'

'Of course, my boy. It will be a change for me to eat in.'

After another Fortnum & Mason game pie – Mrs Higgins was ill again – I told him about Cromer and our plans for 'The Hound of the Baskervilles'.

Doyle and I were to travel to Dartmoor on a research trip. Staying with my parents in Ipplepen would allow us to explore the south-eastern quadrant of the moor. We would then move on to Rowe's Duchy Hotel in Princetown: Doyle was keen to visit nearby Dartmoor Prison where, some years before, without ever having seen the place, he had set one of his Brigadier Gerard stories, 'How the King Held the Brigadier'. We planned to be away for just over a week.

'It is all quite astonishing,' said my uncle. 'What do your parents make of it?'

'I haven't told them yet. In fact, on the subject of telling, it would be better to keep this quiet for now.' I did not want Doyle to think I was boasting to all and sundry.

'Of course. I quite understand – and as you know I am discretion itself. What I *don't* understand, I must admit, is the title: "The Hound of the Baskervilles".'

'What do you mean?'

'It sounds rather gothic. Not in Doyle's style at all.'

'Perhaps that is my corrupting influence.'

'Will there be family curses? Persecuted maidens?'

I took a sip of claret. 'Both, conceivably.'

John O'Connell

Uncle John's sigh had a dying fall. 'Everywhere I look people are reading Stoker's "Dracula". How can that be when it came out four years ago?'

'There is a new cheap edition with a soft cover. Abridged, so I'm told.'

'Is that right? Fancy Irving's factotum having a literary success! Tell me, will your book have vampires?'

'No,' I said, though in truth I had not thought about it one way or the other.

'What will it have then?'

'Mist.'

'I dislike mist. What else?'

'A hound,' I said. 'It will definitely have a hound.'

'As long as you are kind to it, Bertie. You will be kind to the hound, won't you?'

'"The Hound of the Baskervilles". It's a good title, I'll give you that.' Pearson broke off to light his pipe. 'So how is it going to work, this collaboration? Will you write one line and Doyle the next?'

'I don't know,' I said.

'Better find out.'

'I intend to.'

'Before you go, I mean. Have the conversation.

Actually, do more than that. Draw up a contract.'

'Why?'

'To quantify your input. And protect your investment.'

'You make it sound like economics.'

'It is economics. But then I would say that, I'm a publisher.'

'Writing doesn't work like that.'

'It ought to.'

'If I presented Doyle with a contract, well… I don't think he'd sign it, to be perfectly honest.'

Pearson shrugged theatrically.

I felt my patience draining away. 'What is that supposed to mean?'

'Do you know,' said Pearson, 'the one foreign phrase I feel sad we can't use is *primus inter pares*. It has a wider application than English politics.'

'Rewrite your rules, then.'

'Look, Robinson. I'm going to say this once and you must take it how you will. Doyle is one of the most famous and successful writers in the country. You are not. Whatever this… arrangement entails, you are not going into it as equal partners. So you are unlikely to emerge from it as equal partners. If that does not worry you, well, fine. But you are ambitious, I can see that. You have an agenda, as a writer and as a man.'

'What, then?' I asked. 'What should I do?'

'Go, by all means. But keep your eyes open. And get him to write something for us.' Pearson winked at me. 'A new Holmes story, perhaps?'

I turned left out of the station, as instructed by Gladys. I climbed the hill and passed through the long, sunny village street. Then came the sharp turn to the right, the unmade track, the tall chestnut trees, the locked gate.

I knocked on the door of a thatched cottage, again as instructed, and a friendly old woman came bustling out with a key. She was careful to lock the gate behind me.

The house lay about a mile further along the track. It was a large cottage, its roof slated, its granite walls newly whitewashed. From the garden, where the cherry trees were beginning to bloom, came the soothing hum of bees. The sun was bright and unexpectedly hot.

Gladys was sitting in a deckchair by a high wall covered in a climbing hydrangea. She wore a summer dress of light cotton. She looked up from her book as I approached. Spun-gold hair tumbled down her shoulders.

Shielding her eyes from the sun's glare, she said: 'So you found it.'

'I almost didn't.' I dragged a stool across from the porch and sat next to her. 'It's beautiful.'

'I know.'

'You still won't tell me who owns the house?'

She shook her head.

'Do I know him?'

'Her.' She smiled. 'No, you don't. I used to act with her. She is very successful now, on the stage. You would certainly have heard of her. She lets me come here, when I need to get away from London. When I need to be on my own. The only condition is that I tell no-one where I have been.'

'Not even your father?'

'I did tell him once.'

'And now you are telling me.'

'I want you to know.' She looked at me intently. 'I want you to know everything, in time. We will talk properly, when you return from Dartmoor.'

'Gladys,' I said. I leaned across and took hold of her arm. It was soft and warm to the touch. She did not withdraw it.

Our breathing became fast. I felt the throb of her pulse, the whole uncoiled current of her body passing into me, emptying itself into my veins.

Her breath on my cheek was hot and sweet.

She put her lips against my ear and whispered, 'Now.'

Chapter 5

And so we come to the main matter of my story: our trip to Dartmoor, the great wilderness of bog and rock that cuts Devonshire in two. In the interests of accuracy I intend to rely here on the detailed diary in which I recorded my thoughts and impressions at the time.

What follow are essentially my diary entries, embellished in places where I felt more information was called for.

Saturday, May 25th 1901
11am: Arrived in Ipplepen yesterday evening. A full, noisy train on account of this being Bank Holiday weekend. The weather: pleasantly warm and sunny. Frantic preparations were being made for ACD's visit – the best towels put out in his room, much fussing over the menu: 'Does he eat game or will he find it too heavy? Perhaps fish would be better?' etc. It is as if Doyle is royalty. He will be here this afternoon. We could not travel down together as he was committed to a two-day match at Lords.

Father is worse but will permit no 'fussing' or indeed any sort of speculation about his condition. He disappears frequently 'to rest'. Meanwhile, mother and I circle each other warily. She has been reading ACD's works so that she can discuss them with him. I told her he might not wish to discuss Holmes and she said, 'But that is absurd. Besides, he is our guest here. It would be very rude of him to be so sensitive about something so trivial.'

Last night, after dinner, I went to my room and worked on 'The Wolf of the Baskervilles'. I want a rough sketch to show Doyle while he is here. I know he will want changes made and possibly the whole piece rewritten. (I have gone with a wolf over a hound as to my mind wolves are more frightening than hounds – even demonic hounds.) But I am pleased with it, especially my decision to make Addington Peace an ordinary police detective from Scotland Yard. He is a proper character now. He feels real to me in a way that he did not before.

'The Wolf of the Baskervilles' takes place in the present day, in Cromer rather than Dartmoor – I found I could not give Cromer up – and concerns an old family haunted by a spectral she-wolf: the ghost of an old white albino which the sixth earl of Baskerville brought back from

St Petersburg in 1790.

This albino was the earl's favourite creature – until the day it tore out his youngest son's throat, at which point the earl killed it with his bare hands. In my story 'the beast walks still' (!) in the lower gardens of Baskerville Hall.

Peace has something of Holmes' fastidiousness. That I cannot deny. But he is sufficiently different to be worth considering as the lead for our story, and I look forward to proposing him to Doyle.

Sunday, May 26th
7am: I do not know if I have ever felt as low as this. After last night I feel worthless, humiliated. I could sulk like a child, and the greater part of me says I should withdraw at once from this grim charade and return to London. But another part urges caution and restraint; reminds me, like the best referees, that there is still everything to play for.

I look dreadful, with sallow skin and pin-point pupils – a result of the tiny quantity of laudanum I drank to help myself sleep. In a few hours' time we leave for church and I have not yet shaved or breakfasted. So I must write quickly.

Baskerville collected Doyle from Newton Abbot and brought him here shortly before 6pm.

He seemed well – stouter, a touch of red in his
nose and cheeks. I had forgotten the power of
his charm. He tore through the house, shaking
hands, twinkling at my mother, signing whatever
was pushed his way.

Ned, the stable-boy, came up to say hello, and
the new maid, Phyllis. I did not even know that
she could read.

I was the last to be greeted. The friendly force
with which he shook my hand suggested he had
been saving the gesture up. He winked at me,
grinning broadly, and stage-whispered, 'I was
thinking, on the train...'

'Yes?' I said.

'Our story needs a masterful central figure.
Someone who can influence the whole course of
events.'

'I agree,' I said, pleased that he had raised
the subject. 'In fact, I was going to suggest...'

But he interrupted me. 'And I thought: why
on earth should I invent such a character when I
already have one in Holmes?'

I could not believe what I was hearing.
Really, I felt as if someone had punched me in
the stomach.

'Holmes?' I said. 'But you made it clear, on
the boat...'

'I know, I know. But this will be better for

both of us. It's the strangest thing: the antipathy
I felt – it was as strong as hatred. But now that
I have made the decision to resurrect him I feel
quite different. Liberated, you might say. But we
can discuss it later, yes? Food – that's what we
need now. Ah, Mrs Robinson, that colour does
wonders for you...'

And he was off.

Both my parents adored him. And it must
be said, Mrs Saxham's meal was a triumph –
mulligatawny soup followed by poached salmon
hollandaise and then Cabinet Pudding with jam
sauce. Club fare, the sort of food Doyle loves.

How hard I tried, not to let my disappointment show. And ironically Doyle went out of his
way during the meal to emphasise the collabora-
tive aspect of our project, to insist that it would
not, absolutely not, be a case of him calling the
shots. With my help, he said, he hoped to do a
'proper job' on the research front, as in the past
– I suppose he had in mind 'Silver Blaze' – he
had got upon dangerous ground where he had
taken risks through his want of knowledge.

My father took this as a cue to lecture us all
on the history of Dartmoor.

'It is a fascinating place,' he said. 'No part
of England has so many antiquities in so small a
compass.' Of course, he added, it would take a

lifetime to appreciate properly the various hut settlements, stone circles, kistvaens and rude crosses. But three or four days was long enough for the more intelligent tourist to form a decent impression.

'The dangers can be summed up in two words,' he went on. 'Mist and mire. You can spot the mire by the bright green moss that veneers its surface. The mists are another thing entirely. I know people who have had to spend all night on the moor, not daring to move lest they lose their way.'

My mother asked Doyle if, like Holmes, he felt 'in exile' whenever he left London for the countryside?

He pointed out that he lived not in London but in rural Hindhead on the border of Surrey and Hampshire, an area known as Little Switzerland for its health-giving properties. His newly built house had been cut into the side of a hill so that it was overshadowed by a grove or 'shaw' of trees – hence its name, Undershaw. He explained that he shared this house with his wife, Louisa, and their two children, Mary and Kingsley – 'But if you are asking, "Can one become isolated from society in the countryside?" then the answer is yes.'

My father nodded. 'And the result is that we

live among "poor ignorant folk who know little of the law" – as Holmes puts it so well.'

'Indeed,' said Doyle, who was never embarrassed by having his work quoted back at him.

The conversation moved on to Louisa's illness. My father knew something of the treatments for tuberculosis. The benefits of a solution of quinquina, opium and hydrochloric acid were briefly debated before Doyle's tone grew faltering and personal. He began to talk about Louisa, in much more detail than I had heard him talk before.

'At first,' he said, 'I thought it was a cold that she had been unable to shake off. Then came the loss of weight, the general weakness. She drinks only beef tea and broth. It is hard to...' He broke off, as if conscious of straying too far into private territory. 'Expectorated matter she catches in a handkerchief which she folds up and places under her pillow. But then it becomes dry and turns to dust, infecting the bedclothes, the atmosphere and so the whole room.

'It is the children I worry about. As much as Touie, I mean. Obviously I worry about her. But so little is known about heredity – about its influence on susceptibility. Some say the children of consumptive parents possess enfeebled powers of resistance compared with those whose parents have not been so... tainted.'

'You make it sound like a curse,' I said.

He turned to face me. 'It is a curse. This vile bacillus – it's a form of ancestral blight, a contamination of the bloodline which cannot be halted.'

'At least not yet,' said my father. 'But scientists are making great strides. In the field of tuberculosis, as in... so many other fields.'

A terrible gloom clouded his face, as if some secret sorrow were forcing its way out. For a moment I assumed he must be thinking of little Alice. But of course he wasn't. He was thinking about himself and his own mysterious condition.

Doyle and I caught up properly in the drawing room afterwards. My mother had gone to bed, my father to his study to read. We sat in the gathering darkness, the fire's crackle our only company.

'So, then,' I said, crisply. 'The resurrection of Sherlock Holmes.'

'Yes.' Doyle ran a finger around the rim of his glass. 'You seemed nonplussed when I suggested it. As if you had other ideas.'

I was surprised he had noticed this. And in truth I did not know how honest to be. To accuse him of being bullying and dictatorial would have been pointless – unless the point was to scupper the project. But I did say that such an important decision as this should be debated rather than forced through unilaterally.

'I take your point,' he said. 'The problem in this case is that I have already written 30,000 words of the story. And Holmes is already the star.'

There was an awkward silence as I tried to suppress my anger.

'I thought you would be pleased,' Doyle protested. 'You realise how much attention his return will attract?'

'I do.'

'And how much more the *Strand* will be willing to pay as a result? The extra money will be welcome, I must say. We're having an electric generator installed at Undershaw. They're terribly expensive, even the basic ones are well over...'

'May I read what you have written so far?'

'Ah. I would prefer not, if you don't mind. In a few days, perhaps – when I've had a chance to refine it. As it stands it is really very rough, and there is much latent within it which may never bubble to the surface.'

All right, I said, summoning all my powers of tolerance. But would he at least do me the kindness of reading what I had written?

'Of course,' he said, brightly. 'It would be a pleasure.'

I handed him the manuscript, which I had brought down before dinner. I got an oil lamp and placed it on the table next to him. When he saw the title he spluttered and coughed so violently I worried he was having a heart attack.

'"The Wolf of the Baskervilles",' he managed, once the fit had passed.

'Yes,' I said.

'I don't understand.'

'Wolves are more frightening than hounds. In my opinion.'

'Hmm,' he said.

While Doyle read, I closed my eyes and tried not to imagine his reaction to individual scenes. But it was difficult, for I was in a state of some nervous agitation.

Would he find my opening paragraph arresting? – *It was on the afternoon of December 24th that I stepped from the train at the little station of Cromer. Fresh snow had fallen, and the wind came bitterly over the frozen levels of the fen country.*

Would he admire the precision of my descriptions? – *From the back of the house to the edge of the sea cliffs, a distance of some quarter of a mile, ran an irregular avenue of firs with clipped yew walks and laurel-edged flower gardens on either hand.'*

And what about the moment – the charged, vital, hideous moment – when the narrator finally confronts the ghostly wolf? – *'It was never nearer to me than fifty yards, and the stars gave a shifty light. Yet it left me with an impression that it was about four feet in height and of a dull white colour...'*

Doyle chuckled once or twice which heartened me. At one point he inhaled sharply as if shocked by what he had read. But then he sighed; and tutted; and tutted again.

He laid down the manuscript. He rubbed his eyes, yawning loudly.

'Well?' I asked.

'It is nicely written,' he said.

'Thank you.'

'I enjoyed it very much.'

My heart was racing, I confess. 'Good,' I said.

But then he frowned. 'You have set it in Cromer. So the name Baskerville carries no weight. I thought we agreed on Dartmoor?'

I said that I hadn't realised this was set in stone.

Doyle allowed this excuse. But he added: 'I am not altogether convinced by the ending.'

Now, this was the type of critique for which I had braced myself. I resolved not to react ungraciously. 'Oh?' I said, as casually as I could manage. 'Which aspect of the ending, particularly?'

'Tell me if I have this right. Baron Baskerville is killed and everyone in the household suspects the ghostly wolf. However, the culprit turns out to be not a wolf or indeed any kind of animal, but a naked man bent double and thus obtaining the cover of a nearby hedge.'

'You have it right,' I said.

'I thought I did. It doesn't work, does it?'

'Doesn't it?'

'No.'

'Why not?'

'Because a ghostly wolf doesn't look anything like a naked man.'

'You are ignoring the context,' I said. 'The terrible weather. The general confusion. The narrator is quite befuddled.'

Doyle snorted. 'He would have to be pretty befuddled, wouldn't he?'

'Stop it,' I said, my voice trembling. 'You are mocking me, Doyle. I think that I have deserved better at your hands.'

My outburst evidently shocked him. 'My dear fellow,' he began, 'I beg that you will forgive me if I have seemed harsh. It is only that I regard you as an equal. For this reason I am as rigorous and unsparing with your work as I would be with my own. If we are to work together successfully, well – I don't see how it can be any other way.'

'If we are to work together successfully, you must show me what you have written so far. You must consult me on matters of style, plot and character.'

Doyle absorbed this in silence; then nodded once. 'Very well,' he said. 'It is a deal. I can't pretend it pleases me. But as you have been brave enough to expose your weaknesses to me, I must expose mine to you. Tomorrow I will select the least bad portion of what I have written and let you read it.

'Now,' he rose from his chair, 'let us go to bed so that we can wake in the morning as friends – and equal partners.'

So there we have it – our first argument! I am sure it will not be our last and indeed I would not want it to be. For as the Chinese say, a gem cannot be polished without friction.

That is all for now. The scent of grilled bacon summons me downstairs...

5.30pm: I have come to my room, ostensibly to ready myself for dinner. But there is time to set down my thoughts/impressions of the day so far.

Baskerville

The situation between Doyle and myself is much improved. From the moment we sat down for breakfast it was as if nothing had happened. He noticed my unhealthy appearance and asked if I was all right. I said that I was and it was not mentioned again. My father looked stern. Has he noticed my theft of his laudanum? I forgot to top the bottle up with water.

Doyle came to church with us, to the 10 o'clock service. My father was concerned about the local reaction – Doyle's interest in the occult (spiritualism, psychical research, etc) is well-known – but it passed without incident. It gave me more pleasure than I expected, showing him a place that had meant so much to me, and where I had once spent so much time. He was particularly impressed by the rood screen, which (I explained) survived Cromwell only after all the figures on it had been covered in black paint.

I lost him for a short while after the service. I supposed he had been talking to the rector – generally, he was much in demand: a little queue formed, of parishioners bearing his books for signing – but then I found him wandering in the church-yard, writing in a little note-book. I imagine he was looking on the gravestones for local names to use in our story. He could have asked me – after all, I gave him 'Baskerville'.

After the service I showed him around Ipplepen. It was very still and quiet on account of it being Sunday.

The weather today has been showery and overcast with a distinct chill in the air – very different from yesterday. I hope it picks up by tomorrow. The plan is to visit Bovey Tracey, Hound Tor, et al. Baskerville will take us.

11.15pm: A good dinner tonight (beef) followed by a good chat with Doyle. We discussed what I can only describe as 'creative philosophies'. He said something interesting, that 'the heroic is the essence of adventure'; that 'more permanence has been obtained by embodying the heroic than in any other way'. I agreed, quoting Aristotle's dictum: 'Character gives us qualities, but it is in actions – what we do – that we are happy or the reverse.' Doyle thought this was good.

We talked about Zola, who divides people so starkly. Doyle said that while he admired 'Germinal' for its depiction of the horrors of mining, he regretted more generally 'the disappearance of make-believe' in modern novels. For him, as for me, storytelling has its roots in simple boyish pleasures. 'All you need is a premise,' he said. 'For example – a man going home late at night sees a white hand sticking out of the

black waters of a silent pool. What happened or
is to happen?'

We had tremendous fun conjuring scenarios
out of this.

Most thrilling of all, Doyle gave me some
pages to read. I intend to read them in bed.

I regret my earlier anger towards Doyle and
feel that we are going to produce something of
worth. He has wrung two major concessions
from me: the title will be canine, not lupine; and
the tale must be set on Dartmoor.

('I don't understand,' he said. 'If you felt so
strongly that it should be set on the east coast,
why did you not cancel this trip, knowing its main
purpose was to research Dartmoor locations?'
I could not give a decent answer, for I think at
some level I associated Doyle's visit more with
cementing our friendship than with working on a
story I thought unlikely ever to be written.)

As for how much of my 'Wolf' will finds its way
into our 'Hound' – I cannot say at this stage.

I am pleased by how well Doyle gets on with
my parents. He puts them at their ease so that
even my mother is tolerable when he is around.
Before dinner this evening, while I read the
newspaper, he spent a good half an hour in
my father's study. I suppose that, being a doctor, Doyle was interested in his drug collection.

Certainly, my father would have been pleased to show it off.

No laudanum tonight – so we will see how well/badly I sleep.

Monday, May 27th
6am: I woke at 5.45am. Baskerville was clanking around outside, readying the coach, horses etc. I tried hard but I could not get back to sleep. I had slept poorly in any case – lack of medication – my imagination found it hard to let go of Doyle's material, which I read last night and is breathtaking. Truly, Holmes has returned – though Doyle has framed it as an old case pulled from Watson's papers, so it is not as if he is risen from the dead.

He has given me the first instalment. Doyle's idea of 'really very rough' differs from most people's for the manuscript is remarkably polished – written in a neat, clear hand and with very few amendments.

It starts in classic fashion with Holmes and Watson receiving one James Mortimer MRCS at 221b. (There is the usual business beforehand with Holmes divining Mortimer's profession and personality from a walking stick he has left behind. It is quite excellently done.)

Mortimer reminds them of the death a

few months before of his friend Sir Charles Baskerville in a yew alley outside Baskerville Hall on Dartmoor. Sir Charles, who made his money in South African speculation, was the scion of an old county family. The cause of death is believed to be a heart attack.

Mortimer pulls from his pocket an eighteenth-century manuscript and draws Holmes' attention to a Baskerville family legend. Sir Charles was a direct descendant of the 'wild, profane and godless' Hugo Baskerville, whose awful behaviour at the time of the Civil War led to his death at the jaws of 'a great, black beast, shaped like a hound yet larger than any hound that ever mortal eye has rested upon'.

From then on, the Baskerville family were cursed to die 'sudden, bloody and mysterious' deaths.

As we might expect, rationalist Holmes dismisses the story as interesting only 'to a collector of fairy-tales'. But Mortimer intrigues him by revealing that he noticed footprints upon the ground around the body.

'A man's or a woman's?' Holmes asks.

Mortimer replies: 'Mr Holmes, they were the footprints of a gigantic hound!'

The instalment ends there. I confess I burst out laughing with sheer joy when I had finished

reading – a joy which, briefly, eclipsed all envy.
Later, however, in the middle of the night, I began to brood. Doyle had moulded this tale using clay which I had supplied. The family curse
– that had its origins in the story of Richard
Cabell, which I had told him. The black hound
– well, we had both heard the story of Black
Shuck from the waiter in Cromer. But I was the
one who had made the connection with similar
Dartmoor legends.

I keep telling myself that collaboration does
not have to mean both of us holding the pen. I
should be pleased, should I not, that the story is
so good? I will be credited as its co-author. And
there is still plenty of time for me to exert more
concrete influence.

5.30pm: We had a fair day, weather-wise – 60
F, clear skies, no rain. In his ear-flapped travel-
ling cap Doyle looked amusingly like Holmes in
Paget's drawings. Baskerville kept the horses
going at a brisk pace but was surly and distem-
pered. He said very little to either of us.

We had not told him of our decision to use
his name. Doyle, laughing, whispered to me that
perhaps we should not tell him or he might ob-
ject. 'Still,' he said, 'I have put a coachman in
the second instalment. I have called him a "hard-

faced gnarled little fellow".' At this we sniggered like schoolboys till the carriage shook; though a part of me thought: yes, the second instalment <u>which you have obviously finished but will not let me see</u>.

Our first stop: Bovey Tracey, just seven miles away. I explained some of the history – that it was the ancient inheritance of the Traceys, Barons of Barnstaple, a family implicated in the murder of Thomas Becket. The carriage-road was rough and hard. The horses were tired when we arrived and grateful for their 'pick-me-up' of mash and gin. They need it to cope with the next stage of the journey, the narrow uphill stretch that brings you out onto open moorland.

The wind got up as we climbed Haytor, those great knuckles of rock. But as always it was a marvellous sight at the top – the hills rolling away before us, the belts of undulating tableland dotted with ponies and shaggy cattle. I pointed out Bag Tor and Rippon Tor. The horizon is so blurred it is hard to tell moor from sky. Doyle was intrigued by the remains of the old granite railway – one of many speculations to have failed on Dartmoor.

Mrs Saxham had made us some ham sandwiches. We felt such 'grockles', sitting on the ground with little brown parcels open in front of us, our hands and chins greasy with butter. The sun, when it shone, gave a melancholy light, as if despairing of a landscape it was unable to warm.

Crossing the moor, we passed Saddle Tor on the left and went through Hemsworthy Gate. Here, on the right, close under the wall, Doyle made his first acquaintance with a hut circle.

Tuesday, May 28th
To Widecombe. I had been telling Doyle about Widecombe fair, when the streets teem with ruddled sheep and the inn lays on a handsome meal of cold meats. But he had heard of the place in another context – 'It is the home of the devil, is it not?'

I said it was supposed to be.

He said he would like to see it very much.

On the way I told him of the day in October 1638 when all the folk were in Widecombe Church – 'the cathedral of the moor', etc – and the tower was struck by lightning. A storm swept across the valley, in the midst of which an old woman at Poundsgate saw a man ride up on a coal-black horse. His eyes too were black, and his thick eyebrows met in the middle. He asked her for a drink. She gave him some liquor – and his identity was confirmed by the terrible hissing sound it made as it trickled down his throat. She screamed and fled to the church, but the devil followed her there. He snatched her up and flew with her through the roof of the church tower, vanishing on the wings of the storm.

Doyle liked the church and the whole charming picture that Widecombe makes. The inn, I observed, has expanded since I was last there and now has a lunch and tea room at the back to accommodate excursionists.

We left Widecombe by the north-east road which winds up the hill towards Bell Tor and the road to Manaton. We got as far as Bowerman's Nose but decided not to proceed further as we plan to see Manaton tomorrow when we go to Heatree House.

Doyle is enjoying himself. 'One never tires of the moor,' he said to me. 'It is so vast, so barren, and so mysterious.'

I agreed, but stressed that walkers need a good local knowledge to find their way in such a trackless region, and must be ready to rely on their wits as they might walk a whole day without meeting a single soul.

On our return Doyle asked to be shown around the garden by my mother. For a moment I was surprised. The idea that someone might request to spend time in her company was novel to me. But then I thought, 'A novelist must make it his job to be interested in everything. For he never knows when he might have use for a particular detail or observation.' I heard him admiring her Ragged Robin as they passed beneath my room. I looked down and saw that Doyle had his notebook with him. So it is as I suspected.

Wednesday, May 29th

An awful dream last night: I was in a wooden hut, lying on the stony ground. Flies everywhere, the sound of distressed livestock. An intolerable smell of death. I turned my head and saw a young woman lying next to me. I could not see her face for the flies. Although she was dead her baby was still chewing at her breasts. They drooped from her dress like flowers battered by a storm.

I awoke in tears, unable to rid myself of the image.

En route to Heatree House we stopped at Hound Tor. The rocks are supposed to resemble a pack of dogs in chase. We decided they did, but only just. Where the Heatree Common lane joins the Chagford and Ashburton road we found the spot known as 'Jay's grave' where a maidservant at Manaton Ford farmhouse is said to have been buried (covertly, in the dead of night) after she hanged herself.

Doyle had wanted to see Heatree as he was looking for a model for our Baskerville Hall. But while it is authentic and in a good situation, it is unattractive – a drab two-storey affair painted white. Of course, in a sense we are only looking for elements we can reconstitute into a fictional whole. Doyle has already given the place a yew alley – a detail he says he invented, though it preys on me that the house in my Cromer story has such an alley.

As we turned up the drive, Baskerville broke his silence and came out with a bizarre story about Heatree having once belonged to his family, the Dartmoor Baskervilles.

'To think,' he said, 'I could be lord of this manor rather than coachman to you.'

There followed a certain amount of anguished meditation on the fickleness of fortune which Doyle and I tolerated on the grounds that it was amusing, though the more I think of it I should have scolded him for his damned impudence.

We need the house to be surrounded by trees, but also for the high moor to be visible from its windows. Heatree has none of these qualities. Major Kitson, its owner, gave us tea and answered our questions. He did not know who Doyle was and was initially suspicious. But Doyle won him over with stories about South Africa and offered to send him a copy of his Boer book as a thank-you.

Later, I helped Doyle with some of the plotting. I suggested that Sir Charles's nephew and heir, Sir Henry, should be a Canadian fellow and Doyle agreed. He suggested in turn that I write the chapter where Holmes and Watson meet him at his hotel in London. He has just been sent a threatening letter made up of words from different newspapers cut out and pasted. (This was Doyle's idea.) I intend to work on it tonight, hence this short entry.

Thursday, May 30th
5pm: Terrible weather today. The rain in the night was so fierce I thought the windows would shatter. We have all the fires lit but the cold remains intense.

There is little to report. Doyle and I spent much of the day playing billiards. Doyle wants our hound to be real in the end, not a phantom. He said the glowing effect could be achieved by covering an ordinary hound in phosphorescent paint. I said I was not sure if such a thing existed, and even if it did would it have the desired effect? Doyle said it did not matter and took me to task generally for what he sees as my literalism – for I have been quibbling over specifics, especially where the distance between the various moorland sites is concerned.

'For the tale to work,' said Doyle, 'it will be necessary to make adjustments to the topography so that everywhere important is within easy reach of our Baskerville Hall. You know Dartmoor well – but most people do not. In any case, it does not matter. As Emerson says, "There are no facts, only art."'

I thought of Hex in Patagonia, of how easy it would be for him to invent whole districts and episodes in his Express pieces. Say he claimed to have found the Mylodon – we would only have his word for it. No-one would expect him to whip out a Brownie and photograph it. He could get away with murder.

A letter arrived this morning, from Gladys. She has been to the concert hall at the Crystal Palace to hear Schubert's Unfinished Symphony. A fight broke out afterwards in the shilling tea-rooms, with customers throwing buns and pouring tea over each other. Her account was amused (she is getting better at that – at being amused by the world) but also indignant at the authorities for 'penning in the poor' as if they were animals.

Gladys, it is clear, wants a new and better world. A modern utopia. But increasingly I worry that there is only the old world of primal urges and calculated deceptions. I worry Gladys will be disappointed – not just by me, but by life. Remaking the world requires force as well as intelligence. Holmes can interpret the world, but he cannot change it.

Oh, I do not know why I am thinking these dreary thoughts! Cabin fever perhaps, or a want of exercise.

I noticed this morning that my favourite cufflinks are missing. I must have mislaid them in London as I have not yet worn them down here.

Friday, May 31st
4.40am: The worst dream yet. It made even less sense to me than the others.

I was in a bare room with white walls. A young woman – respectable-looking, thin – was strapped into a chair like a dentist's chair. Two men stood around in police uniforms.

As the woman wriggled and screamed, one of them leaned over and forced her mouth open with his hands while the other passed a flexible tube (of indiarubber?) down her throat. At this the fist which had been hanging by her side unclenched, the fingers splaying to reveal a rosy

weal like stigmata at the centre of her palm.
The sound of her gagging was so loud it almost
drowned out the men's voices. But I heard one
of them say: 'It's a shame you silly women can't
think of something better to do with your exuber-
ance.' Added his companion, chuckling: 'See? It
is not so hard to eat your dinner.'

10pm: A curious day, full of revelation. Our meal
tonight ended early, its tone having grown peculiar, and when we parted it was with the wary
politeness of strangers.

I will come to the meal presently. First,
though, I must place the rest of the day's events
on the record.

The 20-mile journey from Ipplepen to
Princetown took over five hours, including a
stop at Two Bridges to view the hotel. Doyle had
heard it was more comfortable than the Royal
Duchy where we were booked and insisted on see-
ing it despite my protestations. The Wisht Wood
nearby was as underwhelming as I remembered.
There is only an acre left, much of it impassable.
We saw no black dogs.

Princetown is cold and blustery, as you would
expect of a town 1,368 feet above sea level. We
passed the prison on our right on our way up
from Two Bridges – indistinct in fog which

seemed to be belching from its own chimneys. The hotel dates from the early part of the last century. It housed the militia forces guarding the French and American prisoners of war that the prison was built to detain.

The bedrooms are simply furnished but clean. They smell of damp and lavender. Our sitting room looks over the moors at the back of the inn. At night it affords a splendid sight as a great searchlight of moon draws the strange tors in black silhouette upon the luminous skyline.

The funny little dining room was hung with mezzotints. Over dinner, we concocted the idea of an escaped convict who holds the key to the Baskerville mystery. Doyle agreed that I could write this part. (He has, by the by, asked the hotel manager to arrange a tour of the prison tomorrow morning.) We also decided, after much debate, that Holmes would be absent for much of the story. He will be in London, or so he leads Watson to believe, and therefore Watson will do the bulk of the work.

I was unsure about this at first. Why bring Holmes back only to waste your advantage? 'Readers want Holmes,' I said, 'not Watson.'

But Doyle shook his head. 'This is Watson's chance to shine! To show what he can do!'

Baskerville

The evening seemed to be proceeding along normal lines. But then – I am not sure why; I suppose something must have prompted it – I started to tell Doyle about a pupil at my school who had died; not a friend exactly, but a class-mate. A horse kicked him in the back of the head. I was six at the time. It was my first experience of the death of a direct contemporary and made, as you might imagine, a strong impression.

Doyle listened sympathetically. Then he asked me – very gently, as one might ask a child – if I believed in life after death.

I said I did not know. Who among us could presume to know such a thing?

He told me what I already knew: that he believed not just in an afterlife but that it was possible <u>for the dead to commune with the living</u>. He said he wished newspapers would be less cynical about spiritualism: 'They don't want it to be true. They want to unmask frauds. To suggest that all mediums are fraudulent. Some are, of course. But that doesn't mean you can damn them all. And even some of the mediums who have been caught faking – they weren't ac-tually fakes. They were faking to demonstrate a broader truth.'

I must have looked confused because Doyle went on: 'It is like a journalist faking an account of a battle or a siege. You were telling me about it, on the Briton. "Magic carpeting" – that was the phrase you used.

'Newspapers owe it to their readers to lay out the facts about spiritualism. I want them to look again at what they have done, at the innocent people they have libelled. You have to understand: all modern inventions and discoveries will sink into insignificance once the facts about spiritualism are fully known.' Doyle paused. 'Do you remember Arthur Coddling?'

'The name is familiar.'

'He was – is – the greatest medium of his age. But his reputation was destroyed, by newspapers. He was driven out of England and now lives in Russia where his talents are appreciated.'

This last detail jogged my memory. Coddling, I recalled, was a physical medium specialising in materialisations. He had been very successful, sitters raving especially about the results he obtained from so-called 'slate-writing', whereby spirits communicate via two slates fastened together using a pencil that has been placed between them.

Six or seven years ago, however, Coddling was targeted by the Society for Psychical Research on account of his involvement with Madame Blavatsky, of whom you will have heard.

The Society sent an investigator along to a sitting. His report declared Coddling's mediumship to be 'simply conjuring'. The outcry was predictable, and exacerbated by the interest of the fledgling *Daily Mail*.

I said: 'So you are saying Coddling was treated unfairly by the press?'

'I am saying,' said Doyle, 'that there is a state I call the "half-trance condition" – really, it is hard to explain to a lay person – when a medium cannot be held responsible for his actions because his higher faculties have ceased to work. In this state he may behave... peculiarly.'

'Peculiarly?'

Doyle sighed his impatience. 'It may look as if the medium is cheating. But he is not. Of course,' he looked away, 'I would not expect the *Daily Mail* to understand the nuances of the case. It would take a different sort of newspaper. An altogether better class of newspaper.

'I must say, I have been impressed by Hex's dispatches in your *Express*; also the open-mindedness and intellectual generosity of the editor who commissioned them.'

I wanted to say, 'It wasn't me! It was Pearson!' and point out that whatever Hex's intentions Pearson was more interested in tickling the public with mumbo-jumbo than serious enquiry.

But I did not. For there it was, as clear as the sky in August: what Doyle was driving at; what was required of me; why I had been courted and asked along on this ludicrous feint of a trip.

It had nothing to do with 'The Hound of the Baskervilles' and everything to do with finding a patsy, a plant, a friend in Fleet Street who would be sympathetic to the cause.

I was so angry that I was unable to say anything.

'You doubt me,' said Doyle. 'I see that. But you shouldn't. You mustn't. A closed mind means an earthbound soul. Besides, I think you may be psychic yourself.'

'Nonsense,' I said, sharply, wiping my mouth, preparing to rise, to put not just this evening but the whole venture behind me. 'What on earth gives you that idea?'

'The dreams you have.'

I felt the blood drain from my face. My heart began to pound, my breathing to become heavy and stertorous. I asked, 'How do you know about my dreams?'

'You mustn't be scared,' said Doyle, leaning into the table. 'The spirits know everything. They are watching over us all the time.'

I said, as if to myself: 'How could you know? I have never told you.'

'Tomorrow,' said Doyle, 'we will visit the prison. We will visit Fox Tor mire. Then, in the evening, I will introduce you to someone who will <u>change the way you see the world</u>.' His eyes were gleaming. 'You will be at the vanguard of the modern. Isn't that what you want? Isn't that where you always wanted to be?'

Chapter 6

So great was Doyle's confidence in his powers that I am sure he believed, after we had shaken hands and retired to our rooms, that the matter was closed. But it was not.

I felt exploited, fatally charmed. *This is what happens,* I told myself. *This is the consequence of being so deucedly good-natured.*

Who was this person who would 'change the way I saw the world'? With that very phrase Gladys had introduced her pet revolutionary – the straggly Russian fellow in the leather jerkin. I was always being promised audiences with such people, as if my perception were uniquely aberrant; as if I personally were holding the world back through a refusal to open my mind to – what? Nonsense, most of the time.

As for my dreams: how had Doyle known about them? Was there truth in his talk of 'psychic powers' or had he simply heard me crying out in my sleep, as I suppose I must have done? (Our rooms at the hotel were adjacent, though they had not been in Ipplepen.)

Baskerville

My brain buzzed with these and other questions.

I slid out of bed and over to the table by the window. The weather was cold for the time of year and I was glad of the thick socks I had brought to walk in.

I lit the lamp. The light it cast through its green shade was wonderfully soothing – a little pool of peace. I forgot my longing for a fire and was able to concentrate on my work.

First, I opened my diary and wrote my account of the day, the account you read in the previous chapter. Then I took out my notebook and started to sketch out a plot for my own Dartmoor story. I decided much of the action would take place here – not just in Princetown, but in this very hotel.

My pen slid across the paper in great scrambling strokes. Within minutes I had the basic architecture mapped out.

I sat back, stretched out my legs, cricked my fingers. This was easy.

Obliging fellow that I am, I had handed over to Doyle my foolscap contributions to what I now thought of as 'his' 'Hound of the Baskervilles'. As yet he had not said whether they pleased him or chimed in any way with what he was writing. Perhaps it was not the great author's style to give feedback. Or perhaps – more likely, given what I now knew of him – he was forging on regardless, mindful of his needs alone.

No question, Doyle's behaviour had diminished him in my eyes.

I was very angry that night. But I am ashamed now of the bitter things I wrote in my diary, on pages I subsequently tore out and destroyed lest they be read by someone who did not understand the context.

I wrote that Doyle was not a great writer, just an ordinary one who had struck lucky. Sherlock Holmes was not so very original – an idiot could see that he was one part Monsieur Lecoq to two parts C Auguste Dupin. And was it not the measure of the man that Doyle was so happy to use others' ideas when it suited him? Why, he had even bought a plot from me, one he would go on to use in 'The Adventure of the Norwood Builder'.

I wrote that it was ludicrous for Doyle to hate Holmes when Holmes had given him so much, not least a willing readership for his other, lesser works.

And I wrote awful things about Jean Leckie, things I cannot bring myself to repeat.

I am not a jealous person, nor have I ever hankered after wealth or privilege. But I am competitive – fiercely so. This explains the urge that suddenly overcame me: to beat Doyle at his own game, on the same turf, using the same bat.

Baskerville

From the material we had gathered in the course of our trip, material intended for 'The Hound of the Baskervilles', I would create another story every bit as terrifying and ingenious – and every bit as successful.

Saturday, June 1st

We rose early for our prison visit and were eating breakfast (eggs, kippers, coffee) by 6 o'clock. Yesterday's newspapers had arrived from Plymouth and we read them as we ate. Doyle read aloud, at length, from an editorial in *The Times* on the slave trade in East Africa. He seems not to notice awkward atmospheres – perhaps because he is so confident of obliterating them?

I should have been tired, having stayed up so late writing. But my new ambition was a vitalising force. It made me blush to think of it, like a guilty secret.

The prison governor collected us from the hotel's smoking room. A short man with a thin moustache, he wore a dark suit of respectable antiquity, put on I suspect for our benefit, or rather Doyle's, for within minutes he had declared his love for Sherlock Holmes and even 'The White Company'. He asked Doyle if it was true he was thinking of resurrecting Holmes; he had heard a rumour to this effect.

Doyle winked and said that he would have to wait and see.

The prison is a large and imposing place. A chill went through us as we wandered beneath the great granite archway with its lofty inscription (*parcere subjectis* – 'spare the vanquished') and into the forecourt where a scattering of prisoners loitered silently. They stared at us with that gormless curiosity which results from a monotonous and purely animal existence.

The prisoners live in tiny iron cells whose only light comes from a tiny window set high in the wall. We were permitted to peer through a spy-hole in the door to one of the cells. There was a palpable weight in the atmosphere, an undefined, brooding menace, and we were fearful of what we might see. In the dim light of a lamp held up to a window beside the door, I made out a mattress resting upon an iron frame sunk into the wall at the head and foot. There was no other furniture in the place, not even a chair.

I heard a scratching sound. The governor said this was most likely a rat gnawing in the wall: 'Their little teeth work away at the mortar between the bricks.'

We were shown around the mess and saw the

work parties marching off to the quarries and enclosures, their pallid faces resigned to the deadening routine. Guards armed with carbines and bayonets followed close behind.

It is a brutal place. Last year, the governor said, they gave out 566 punishments for offences ranging from murderous attacks to idleness and indecency. Doyle asked what sort of punishments and got the reply: 'Leg irons, handcuffs. We might put men in straitjackets or use the old ball and chain. Solitary confinement is a good one, likewise a bread and water diet.'

Flogging with a cat o' nine tails – anywhere between 24 and 36 lashes is the norm – leaves scars on the back for life, but is preferred to birching as that is held to be more humiliating.

Upon admission, inmates are supplied with new boots. Outside workers in the bogs get two pairs, as well as an extra suit of clothes and a blue and red striped jacket called a slop. Heads and beards are clipped close, as close as scissors are able. One full bath is permitted per fortnight.

After he had told us this the governor turned to me and said, 'I hear you are a local man.'

I said that I was, that I knew the area well and felt foolish for not having visited the prison before. I asked him if it was not the case that the convicts' outdoor work – draining and enclosing portions of moorland – afforded them an excellent chance of escape, especially if a fog came down suddenly.

He shrugged. 'In a city a man may vanish in a crowd, but on Dartmoor he must tramp a dozen miles before he can find even a bush to hide him.'

Doyle saw me writing all this down in my notebook and whispered, 'Excellent work.'

I smiled, but it was a guilty smile – for I was making the notes not for 'The Hound of the Baskervilles' but for my own tale, which I have decided to call 'The Mystery of Thomas Hearne'.

Afterwards, we returned to the Duchy to change into our walking clothes. The hotel kitchen had made us beef sandwiches which we packed into our ruck-sacks before setting off in the direction of Two Bridges. We turned right at the Methodist chapel onto the track that leads to the old tin mines at White-works and hence the impassable bog of Fox Tor mire.

Fox Tor is truly remarkable – a thousand acres of quaking slime, in any part of which a horse and rider might disappear, never to be seen again. The bright green patches are treacherous sphagnum moss: deceptively beautiful, fringed with marsh flowers and pale pink heather.

To avoid Fox Tor mire we kept along on the

slope of the hill to the right of it. About a quarter mile to the northward of it is Childe's Tomb, where an old hunter is supposed to have perished after losing his way. It was so cold (the legend goes) that he killed his horse, disembowelled it and climbed inside its belly to get heat. But it was not enough to preserve him and he froze to death.

Doyle wanted to see the prehistoric stone huts at Grimspound as he has an idea that Holmes will hide there in his story. I found it useful for my 'Thomas Hearne' too.

We were exploring the interior of one of the huts when suddenly we heard a boot strike against a stone and rose together. It was only a lonely tourist on a walking excursion, but at the sight of our heads emerging from the hut he let out a yell and bolted. We both sat down and rocked with laughter, any antagonism between us briefly a distant memory.

All told we covered some 14 miles on foot and returned to the Royal Duchy at 5pm, sore and weary. Doyle said how useful he had found the day and I felt a burst of sorrow in my chest that a collaboration conceived in hope should have ended in this way.

Doyle said he had some letters to write and set off towards the staircase. As he crossed the lobby he was intercepted by the manager, who led him into a narrow room behind the reception counter. I stayed where I was, sorting through the things in my ruck-sack.

When finally Doyle emerged he came over to me, and I thought I smelled something on his clothes, some coarse fragrance like patchouli oil. In a low voice, so as not to be overheard by the party of hikers to our left, he said: 'I have arranged to eat in my room tonight. Will you join me?'

'Of course,' I said. 'But why?'

No sooner had I raised my hand to rap on the door than Doyle answered. He beckoned me in, then put the same fingers against his lips to shush me.

'What is this?' I whispered. 'What is going on?'

The room, which was bigger than mine, had a peculiar charge, as if something of the magnetism of its occupant had diffused in it.

Except that there was more than one occupant: Doyle, obviously; but also a woman sitting in the corner on an antimacassered red silk chair.

She was facing the wall, like a child being punished. Her curly brown hair hung loose. It trailed over her shoulders and down her back. I edged forward so that I could see her profile and was rewarded with a glimpse of a full nose and protuberant lips. Her eyes were shut. Indeed, she seemed to be in a sort of contemplative trance.

In truth it was hard to see all that much. The curtains were drawn and the only light came from two candles placed on a circular deal table at the foot of the four-poster.

The blazing fire cast shadows like capering animals on the wall opposite. 'The spirits dislike the cold,' Doyle explained. I thought: I don't like it either, but when *I* asked the manager about lighting a fire I was told the hotel had run out of wood.

Only two places had been laid at the table, though there were three chairs. I sat down next to Doyle. 'Is your visitor not joining us?'

He shook his head. 'The spirits dislike food.'

Our dinner – beef again – had arrived already and was being kept warm in two silver chafing dishes. There was no wine: 'The spirits disapprove...' etc.

I said, 'Why do you keep on about spirits? And who is that woman?'

'She is Madame D'Esperance, Britain's most accomplished medium. We are going to have a séance.'

'What? Conjure the dead? Here?'

'Here will do fine.'

'Will it work?'

'If the atmosphere is right. There must be no frivolity. An earnest, prayerful atmosphere puts the spirits at ease.'

I looked again at the woman. 'Why is she sitting like that?'

'She is readying herself. Making herself... open.'

We ate in silence. When we had finished Doyle collected up the things and put them on a tray outside the door, for he had left instructions that we should not be disturbed.

Then he spread out on the table a selection of *cartes de visite*. 'You should look at these,' said Doyle. 'They give an idea of the results Madame D'Esperance can achieve.'

One by one I picked them up and squinted at them in the low, jumping light.

The composition of each of the photographs was identical: a man or woman sitting stiffly upright on a plain wooden chair. Next to them, hovering in the air, were shadowy forms. Mostly these forms resembled blotches where liquid might have been spilled on the paper. But the better examples showed doll-like apparitions with mask-like faces. In one or two the conjured spirit was so human-looking that I confess the hairs on my neck stood up.

I had seen such photographs before, of course. We were sent them frequently at the *Express* by spiritualists who wished us to publish them. No-one in the office took them very seriously.

Doyle bade me examine them closely, until I was convinced no trickery was involved. I could not say how the effect had been produced – I am no expert in these matters – but something about them did not look right to me and I said as much.

Doyle did not mind. He could explain the science behind them, as he could explain most things.

'The photographic plate is sensitive to dark light which the human eye cannot detect. The spirits have an etheric or radiant body. They use the terrestrial molecules that surround them in order to build up a material body capable of manifesting itself to our senses.'

'I see.'

'Think of it in terms of wireless telegraphy.'

'I'm doing my best.'

'Your scepticism is natural. Everyone is sceptical, initially.'

I asked: 'How involved is Louisa in all this?'

Doyle sighed heavily. 'One of the great sadnesses of my life is that she does not want to hear about it. It upsets her, in her present condition. Although it shouldn't. It should remove the fear, not increase it.'

'And Jean?'

'She listens to my lectures. But I have not yet...

inducted her, if that is the word.' He looked at his watch. 'Goodness,' he said, 'it is later than I thought. We must begin.'

Together we approached the seated woman. Her serenity was absolute, as if she would not know how to act otherwise.

Doyle rested a hand on her shoulder. He stooped and whispered at her ear, 'Madame, may I introduce my great friend, Bertram Fletcher Robinson.'

It thrilled me, still, to be described in this way.

The arm she extended seemed unnaturally long. Her proffered hand felt cold and damp. I did not know what to do with it, it was not like the hand of an ordinary woman; so I squeezed it lightly before letting it drop.

Her gleaming blue eyes looked deep into mine. Her skin was clear and smooth. It was hard to say her age – perhaps 50? Her mouth hung open so that I could see her tongue quivering and glistening. Her breath smelled of dead geraniums.

'He was right,' she said, in a voice like gossamer. 'He was right!'

'Who?' I said, turning from the woman to Doyle. 'What does she mean?'

'You have the gift,' said Madame D'Esperance. 'Dr Doyle said he thought you were unusually sensitive.'

'I don't know about that,' I said, shruggingly.

'I was showing him the photographs,' said Doyle.

Madame D'Esperance smiled like a happy child. 'Ah yes. Spirit photography is such a gift. It helps us understand matter and force – how they can merge into one another.'

'They are quite remarkable,' I said. 'Tell me, how does one photograph a ghost?'

'With a magnesium flare,' said Doyle, as if this was widely known.

'The flash only lasts an instant,' said Madame D'Esperance. 'The spirits do not mind it.'

Later, I would realise that I had read about this woman somewhere. But I did not know at that stage what I am about to tell you. That her real name was Elizabeth Hope; that she had published a book, 'Shadow Land', a few years before; that she had several famous 'spirit guides', the most celebrated of whom was a young Arab girl, Yolande.

During séances the materialised Yolande would wander freely among the guests and flirt with the men in the audience. She was a complete innocent in our world; she did not even know how to sit on a chair. But people will always take advantage of innocence, and one day a man driven mad with lust by Yolande's immodest attire succeeded in touching her most private parts.

The consequences can be imagined. Yolande

dematerialised on the spot, while 'ectoplasmic impact' caused Madame D'Esperance's lungs to rupture in a single rapid contraction.

She nearly died.

This had happened several years before our meeting, since when Doyle had been in regular contact with her. (I suspect he sent her money, though I cannot prove this.) He had arranged for her to be brought to Dartmoor from Plymouth where she had been living since her return from a successful tour of Russia.

I wondered why Doyle had said nothing to me when he had evidently planned this event weeks ago. Had he worried that I would return to Ipplepen or even London if I found out? Or was it simply that he loved the theatre of secrecy?

He certainly loved theatre. I will never forget the way Madame D'Esperance announced 'I am ready' in a solemn, breathy voice, or the way Doyle escorted her like an invalid from her chair to the table.

Slowly, slowly she walked, as if she were balancing a plate on her head.

Around the uncovered table we seated ourselves, placing our hands on its surface and joining our fingers to make a complete chain. ('It concentrates the spirits' powers.')

We sat there for some time, the silence drawing my attention to the myriad creakings and shufflings

that are the mark of any hotel. Every now and then
Madame D'Esperance twitched and gave a little
shriek – a spastic bit of business that did no more
to convince me of her authenticity than her disor-
dered, gypsy-like appearance.

I looked at the clock above the fire. Half an hour
had passed with nothing to show for it.

Doyle was growing jittery. You are not supposed
to speak during a séance, but he leaned over and
whispered, 'Are you feeling any discomfort? A prick-
ling, tingling sensation? If so, that is quite normal.'

I wanted to say that I felt nothing I could not at-
tribute to cramp and the hardness of the chairs. But
I said thank you, I was feeling fine, etc.

A matter of minutes later, Madame D'Esperance
cried out. The effect on the atmosphere was electric. Doyle's hand gripped mine tightly; likewise the
medium's on the other side, her long nails digging
into the palm of my hand so that my reflexive urge
was to pull away. But I did not break the circle.

Madame D'Esperance opened her eyes and said
dreamily, 'They are here.'

I felt Doyle's pulse quicken. 'Excellent,' he muttered.

'However, they do not wish to materialise. The
energy in the room is not sufficient.'

Doyle's hand relaxed its grip. 'I say,' he said,
'that's a bit of a blow. I was hoping…'

'Wait! A man is here. A bearded man. He is pale and thin. He has a paintbrush in his hand. I am sensing the letter A very strongly.'

Almost immediately Doyle shouted out: 'Altamont!'

I said, 'What is Altamont?'

'My father's middle name. This is my father, no question. He died in '93.'

'Quiet!' commanded Madame D'Esperance. 'You will scare the spirits away!'

'Tell him I am sorry,' Doyle implored. 'I am sorry I was not at his funeral. It coincided with a talk, you see. At the Norwood Literary and Scientific Society. Frederic Myers – he said he had proof. Of man's continued existence after death.'

'Your father forgives you,' said Madame D'Esperance.

But there was hysteria in Doyle's voice and he could not stop himself. 'I had to hear about it. Because if it is true, if there really is life after death, what does a funeral matter? What is the point of grieving? You understand, don't you? Father?'

'Your father bids you farewell,' said the medium.

Doyle cried out: 'No!'

'He has moved on. I have lost contact. Wait – who is this?'

I had been thinking that this was a decidedly amateur production. But then the blue eyes of

Madame D'Esperance looked at me, into me.

'There is a girl here,' she said. 'She has yellow hair plaited into two long tails. She is wearing a light summer frock.'

The room seemed to contract around me. My vision blurred and I felt cold all over.

Later, recollecting the scene in tranquillity, I would see a smile of hard-won satisfaction on Madame's face as she realised her mediation had been successful. But I cannot say for certain that it was there. Who knows what we imagine and what we don't?

All I knew in the delirium of that moment was that Madame's description matched Alice perfectly.

I looked at Doyle. His nostrils flared as his breathing grew thick and convulsive.

But Madame wanted my attention and knew how to get it. 'The girl is called Alice.'

'I know,' I said.

'She was your friend.'

I felt my throat tighten and the tears forming themselves. 'She was.'

'She has a message for your father. That he should not feel guilty about her death. She is happy now, so happy. As he will be, when he too passes over in a few months' time.'

'What?' I said, leaping up. 'How does she know this?'

('Sit down,' said Doyle, squeezing my hand.)

'He has a lump in his belly. It grows a little every day, as if it is eating him from within.' The eyes continued to bore into mine. 'She says she is sorry.'

'For what?'

'That she was so hard to bury. You had to use dynamite to break up the rock. You were injured.'

I nodded. 'I was standing too close. A fragment of rock flew up and cut my forehead.'

'She is kissing the scar. She is too weak to materialise. But I can see her all the same. Her little lips...'

Hot tears were streaming down my face. 'Alice,' I said, softly. 'My Alice.'

'She is opening her hand now.'

I did not know at the time why this troubled me so much, but I said immediately: 'No.'

'She is showing me something.'

'Please, no.'

'Ah!' Madame D'Esperance beamed. 'Of course! It is the brooch you put in her hand. When you buried her. Yes! It is a little gold brooch in the shape of a heart.'

I cried out. For no-one could have known this.

No-one could have known about the brooch, because I had quite forgotten it myself.

Chapter 7

For whatever reason, Alice's spirit chose to loiter – long enough for the shock of its presence to dissipate somewhat. Madame D'Esperance continued to commune with her, but in a fashion that excluded Doyle and me. There was much grunting and tutting, and occasional saying of 'I see' and 'Oh my dear'.

Eventually I tired of it and asked, 'What is she saying?'

Madame D'Esperance had closed her eyes, the better to focus on Alice. When she opened them again there was anger there, a steeliness born of some secret resolve. Oddly, it seemed to be directed at me.

She said, 'Alice is telling me things.'

'What sort of things?'

'I cannot say.'

'Why not?'

She paused. 'They are things you would rather she didn't tell me.'

'What do you mean?' I turned to Doyle, angry now. 'What is she saying? What is she implying?'

'Shhh,' said Doyle. 'You are shouting.'

'Of course I'm shouting.' I pulled my hands free of them both. As I did so, Madame D'Esperance gave a yelp and went limp.

Doyle looked at me in disbelief. 'You have broken the circle,' he said, his voice rising to a whine. 'You have ruined it all, on account of a single spirit being mischievous!'

I said, 'This is very dark mischief.'

Madame D'Esperance had recovered from her faint and was staring at me with hatred. 'Only you could know how dark,' she said. 'Do you deny that the spirit was Alice?'

'I do not know who it was. I could not see anything.'

'Yet you have the gift.'

'I have no gift, Madame.'

'A spirit is controlling you. He is forcing you to deny what is obvious.'

'What did this Alice say to you? What did she say that makes you look at me in this way?'

'You know very well.'

'On the contrary, I cannot imagine.'

'The feelings you had for her…'

'She was my friend.'

'…were vile and base.'

I shrank back, as if struck. 'They were nothing of the sort. You cannot sit there and slander me in this way.' I looked at Doyle, but he would not meet my gaze. 'Help me, Doyle. Defend me. As a friend.'

He coughed, clearing his throat. 'It is not for us to question a spirit's judgement.'

'It is when they are mischievous. You said yourself, the spirit was mischievous.'

'I did not mean...'

'The spirit could have been anyone. Or no-one.'

At this Madame D'Esperance rose from her chair and hissed at me, 'You were seen!'

She froze, realising her mistake immediately.

But I pounced. 'Seen where? Doing what?'

In truth I was asking myself these questions as well as the medium; combing the dusty vault of my memory for a scenario that fitted, a scenario that might yield such intelligence as Madame D'Esperance and Doyle seemed to have at their fingertips.

I realised with horror that it had to be the occasion in the churchyard when I had hugged Alice and kissed her head. There was no other.

But it made no sense to me. That encounter had had about it an innocence so extravagant as to be garish. The determination with which a person would have to twist and stretch to see anything inappropriate in it...

'Answer me,' I demanded, for the medium had gone quiet.

She stalled. 'I cannot say.'

'Did Alice say that we were seen?'

She nodded.

'Liar,' I said. 'Alice could not have known. She was facing the wall. We could only have been seen from the other side, by someone leaving the church. And who would that have been?'

Again, I was asking myself, for I alone was in a position to know the answer. *Had* someone else had been there, someone I had not seen?

It was then that I noticed Doyle look at me, then look away. He was stroking his moustache nervously with his thumb and forefinger. I cannot explain it, but something in his appearance made me suspect him.

'You,' I said. 'What have you been up to?'

'You are very tired,' said Doyle. 'I have thought this for several days now. The creative act is uniquely draining. Perhaps I have driven you too hard. The best thing,' he added quickly, sensing my desire to interrupt, 'the best thing by far, would be for you to turn in for the night. As I always say, a good night's sleep changes the colour of the day.'

I looked at him. 'You say that, do you? Well, I certainly cannot stay here. The whole business makes me sick.'

With that I turned and left the room, slamming the door behind me like an angry child.

Back in my own room, I lay on the bed in my clothes, my whole body tingling. Rage, I have found, puts me in a state of heightened vigilance; no doubt a naturalist could explain it. Through the wall I heard snatches of conversation between Doyle and Madame D'Esperance – the author apologising on my behalf, the medium lamenting the shallowness of my perceptions.

'It was worth a try,' he declared at one point.

'Perhaps,' said Madame D'Esperance.

A few minutes later she left the room. I do not know where she went. Presumably Doyle had booked a room for her.

As I lay there brooding, an image came to me: Doyle, in the churchyard, clutching his notebook. He had told me he was writing down names from the gravestones. But he had also been talking to the Sexton. And – later, in the garden – to my mother.

What had they said to him?

I resolved to find out.

I waited until I heard snoring through the wall. Then I took off my shoes and crept out onto the corridor. Though I did not have far to walk, I timed my steps so that they coincided with the ticking of the clock on the landing.

I stood outside Doyle's room for a couple of minutes, listening, making sure. At one stage his snoring stopped altogether and I thought I would have to go back. But then it started again – a coarse, phlegmy rattling which reminded me of a newborn calf. I rested my hand on the door-knob and turned it, slowly and gently.

The door opened without a sound, as if its hinges had been oiled just for me. The four-poster had its curtains drawn so I could not see Doyle at all.

I held up the lighted candle I had brought with me.

On the far side of the room, by the window, was a mahogany writing desk. I went over to it. But he had left little on it – just a glass of water and a folded newspaper.

Where else might it be?

A huge, convulsive snore gave way to silence.

I froze as the squeaking thump of a large man shifting position on a mattress gave way to… more snoring.

(I should make clear that I was not scared of Doyle. I only sought the freedom to go about my business undisturbed.)

Where was the notebook? In his suitcase? He had left it wide open on the floor. I got down on my knees and put the candle beside me. But its pale light did not reach over the rim, so I had to hold it up with my right hand while my left rummaged away. As a result I spilled several drops of wax on one of Doyle's Gieves & Hawkes shirts.

All for nothing. The notebook was elsewhere.

Under his pillow? His mattress? If so then there was no way I could get at it.

His coat pocket?

I checked. Nothing.

What about the bookshelf? Perhaps he had hidden it in plain sight amid the unread relics of others' holidays?

I traced the books' spines with my finger: several guides to Dartmoor, most of them by Sabine Baring-Gould; 'The Woman in White'; 'Anna Lombard'; 'Three Men in a Boat'. Nothing by Doyle! But nor was there any notebook.

Think, think. Where would he have put it?

My tired eyes fell on the waste-paper basket beside the desk – oak coopered, deep, and oddly full considering it had been emptied that morning.

I went towards it. It was filled with newspaper. But there was a strange uniformity to the size of the balls, as if the pages had been scrumpled up deliberately to pack something out.

I scooped the balls out, handful by handful. And there it was, nestled in the centre: a cheap notebook bought – I could tell – from a station bookstall.

I picked it out, sat down at the desk and put the candle in front of me. Then I flicked through the thing until I came to the most recent entries.

'What is this?' I asked myself. 'What do we have here?'

A few seconds later I had found what I was looking for: a little sketched plan of the church showing it in relation to the churchyard, etc. On the facing page was a description of Alice's grave followed by notes in a very basic, obviously self-taught Pitman shorthand summarising interviews with the Sexton (here 'WB' for Walter Barnes), JFR and someone else, someone with the initials ER.

Emily Robinson. My mother.

The WB interview focused on the death, the laying out, the funeral and the burial of little Alice.

BFR helped me, put brooch in her hand. A lovely gesture. Digging: terribly rocky, dynamite needed... BFR cut on forehead in blast.

The ER one was rather different.

B always a disappointment even as a child – habit of forming unsuitable attachments. Girl in the village, Alice – he saw a lot of her at one time, some thought too much – a sexton's daughter after all. One day at

*the church — as I was leaving I saw them, saw him
kiss her and I knew, I could see, from the way he held
her. They did not know that I was there. Afterwards
I did my best to keep them apart.*

I could not bear to read more. I put the book
down. I sat at the desk for some minutes, adjusting
myself to what I had learned, absorbing its implica-
tions.

Outside the wind howled dolefully as pelting
rain dashed against the windows.

I went over to the bed, pulled back the heavy
curtain that ran along the side — and lo! Doyle
was revealed: crumpled and disarrayed, sprawled
across the bed as if it were a life-raft he had hauled
himself onto. He looked so vulnerable in his
stripy flannel pyjamas. Unmanned. I thought of
Hamlet watching Claudius praying: 'Now might I
do it pat...'

No, no. That would not do. That was not the
solution.

I bent down and shook him by the shoulder until
he stirred. I wish I could say that I shook him gently.
But it would not be true.

Doyle opened his eyes wide and cried out.
'What? Who? Robinson! My God!'

I leaned into his terrified face. 'Wake up, you
blaggard.'

'What is this? It is the middle of the night. For Christ's sake, man!'

'You were going to blackmail me.'

A look of resignation came over Doyle's face as he realised the extent of my knowledge. 'No,' he said. 'Not blackmail.' He sat up and rubbed at his eyes with his fingers.

'What, then?'

'Encourage you. Persuade you to do the right thing. Whatever happened here tonight, the public still needs to know.'

'What? What do they need to know?'

'That death is not the end! The world is changing around us, don't you see? There are no fixed points any more.'

At this black laughter burst from me like water from a siphon. I had not thought of the matter before in these terms, but my views suddenly clarified like a stream cleansed of pollutants.

I said: 'You talk about the vanguard of the modern. Well I have been there. And shall I tell you what I saw? I saw a man on his knees on the floor of a ship's hospital with his arm in another man's chest. I saw blood and shit, panic and fear. I saw the opposite of life, and that is a fixed point whether you like it or not.'

My speech concluded, I looked across again at the desk – and noticed something.

Doyle had left his leather writing case open so that I could see the letter he was working on.

I walked over and picked it up – gingerly, as one might pick up a dead mouse. 'What is this?'

It was addressed to Herbert Greenhough Smith, Editor of the *Strand*.

Doyle raised himself on his elbows. 'That is not for your eyes.'

'It concerns me, though.'

'I repeat,' he said, 'it is not for your eyes.' But he knew it was too late to try to stop me.

I started to read from the letter out loud. ' "I have the idea of a real creeper for the *Strand*. It would run, I think, to not less than 40,000 words. It is just the sort of thing that would suit you, full of surprises, and breaking naturally into good lengths for serial purposes. It would be called 'The Hound of the Baskervilles'.

' "There is one stipulation. I must do it with my friend Fletcher Robinson and his name must appear with mine. I hope that does not strike you as a serious bar. I can answer for the yarn being all in my own style without dilution, since your readers like that. But he gave me the central idea and the local colour and so I feel his name must appear. I shall want my usual £50 per thousand for all rights if you do business." '

Doyle came out fighting. 'That sarcasm in your

tone… You are trying to make the letter sound unfair.'

' "*I* have the idea…" '

'How would it have helped, had I said…'

' "He gave me the central idea and the local colour…"'

'But you did!'

'I also gave you 15,000 words of material! And yet somehow, despite that, you can "answer for the yarn being all in my own style".'

'I would have to have altered it,' he said. 'Ironed out any discrepancies so that the finished work read smoothly. Surely you can see that?'

In a rational frame of mind I am sure I would have reacted differently. But I was not feeling rational.

I went over to him. He stood up so that we were facing each other.

I said: 'You are a thief.'

'If you believe that then I am greatly saddened. It makes a mockery of all we have achieved.'

'Why shouldn't I believe it?'

'For one thing you will be paid. You are being paid, damn it! Who has paid for your dinners and your room here?'

'Me, I had assumed.'

He shook his head. 'I have paid for everything.'

'I never expected that.'

'You will get a share of the royalties as well as the advance. Actually, I was thinking of asking for a higher rate. Does £100 per thousand words sound excessive?'

'This is not about money. It is about respect.'

'Let me assure you, you have earned my utmost respect.'

I laughed incredulously. 'And yet three hours ago you and Widow Twankey made me the butt of some half-witted parlour game.'

'Spiritualism is not a parlour game.'

'Of course it is. You are a fool to believe otherwise.'

At this Doyle grew irate. 'Better a fool,' he said, 'than an insolent journeyman hack.'

I stared at him, my breathing heavy, my heart pounding in my throat. 'Quite so,' I managed, eventually. 'Quite so.'

I turned away, towards the door.

'Wait,' said Doyle. 'Robinson.'

But I did not feel like waiting. I went down the stairs, out of the hotel and across the grey weather-beaten square. Ignoring the hum of voices from the Plume of Feathers inn on the corner, I turned right onto the Yelverton road.

I walked and walked, past the station and the rows of cramped cottages until the moor stretched out before me, black and heavy. It was raining but at that moment I did not feel it: I was angry, and when we are angry we are not conscious of the world around us.

The darkness made everything invisible. But there was a mist, too – thick, growing thicker by the minute.

Even in daylight the Dartmoor mists are disorientating. Small objects close at hand can resemble large ones seen from a distance. I know the moor better than many, but I had with me neither map nor compass: only my wits, and they were not working as they should have been.

I kept on walking, for there is comfort in movement. I did not know where I wanted to go, only where I was likely to end up.

Of what followed I have little recollection, and what I do remember feels like a dream, as if it did not really happen.

I was drenched to the skin and very tired. As I walked and my anger faded I began to imagine hot tea, a bright cosy fire, the welcome of strangers. I knew that I had to keep moving; that eventually, if I followed this road for long enough, I would end up in Yelverton.

But then I saw it: the white figure.

It was perhaps 400 metres to my left and gave off a light so bright and powerful it seemed to burn through the mist.

I stepped off the road and onto the moor. The rocky ground hurt my feet for I was not wearing suitable shoes.

The figure stood there, its arms outstretched towards me. It did not say a word; nor did it seem to breathe – a block of stone could not have been more still. How beautiful it looked in the moonlight!

As I walked towards it I saw with unnatural clarity that it was a young woman. She wore a loose white dress like a robe. Her hair was down and fell about her shoulders. Her face was indistinct yet familiar, and smiling, and infinitely placatory. The sight of it warmed the whole of my body.

She inclined her head, as if in benediction.

I reached out my hand. I needed to touch her, to make sure she was real.

But then, as I was about to touch her dress, she changed.

The face darkened and became livid, the lips retracting so that I could see her clenched teeth. The eyes were wide and staring, the pupils dilated to such a degree that there seemed to be no white at all.

Wild, nauseating fear overcame me and I cried out. At which point the ground, which had been hard, sank beneath my step and I went rolling down, down a steep bank.

I seemed to be at the bottom of a narrow gully.

John O'Connell

I could not get up. Indeed, the slightest movement caused intense pain in my left leg.

The woman was nowhere to be seen. I waited in terror lest she make some effort to find me, but she did not; there was only blackness and pummelling rain. The sheepy smell of mud and wet wool.

And the mist: the mist, draping itself over me.

Chapter 8

I awoke to the sound of voices; the faint, hollow sound that voices make at a distance in a large house. Slowly they became more distinct, melding with the soft thump of footsteps along a wooden corridor.

The creak of a door-handle turning. A voice I knew saying, 'Thank you, Molly. I will take the tray in.' The scrape of metal as the curtains around my bed drew back to reveal an unfamiliar room.

Gladys was there, standing over me.

I spoke her name, decisively, as if it were a charm; then asked: 'Where am I?'

'At a house Doyle has rented. You have been asleep for two days.'

'Doyle,' I said, weakly. 'Where is Doyle?'

'Gone away, just. He brought you here from Park Hill. He was concerned about you. He set your leg, which you broke. After you were found he spent the whole night at your bedside. He read to you for hours, from his own "Micah Clarke". He thought it might rouse you.'

I laughed at this; then winced at the pain, for I

must have bruised a rib when I fell. I said, 'I would have preferred "The Final Problem".'

But Gladys did not smile, nor had she been smiling. Her eyes were red and swollen. 'He has left you a letter. He said it would right things between you. I told him it had better or I would destroy him.'

I wondered what she knew and what she did not. I asked: 'Why am I here and not at Park Hill?'

'I wanted to be with you, but not there. Not after what Doyle told me. I asked him to find us somewhere. Somewhere local, as you could not be moved far. And here we are.'

'It seems nice.'

'It is ours only for another week. We should not get comfortable.'

She sat beside the bed. She was pale and languid from long watching, but still beautiful. I said, 'You have been so good to me.'

'We are engaged. You are ill.'

'But that is my point. There is something I have to say to you. And it breaks my heart. But I cannot possibly marry you, now or at any time.'

'You are wrong,' Gladys said. Of all the responses I had braced myself to expect, it was not this.

'Please. There are facts you do not know about me which make it quite impossible. So it is at an end.'

She said, 'Suppose that I know but do not care?'

She took an envelope from the bedside table and shook its contents into the palm of her hand. There, winking at me, were the cuff-links I thought I had lost. Reading the confusion on my face, she explained: 'Your whore had an attack of conscience.'

'What?' It unsettled me, to hear her use the word so casually.

'She brought them to my door. (You had a *carte* in your pocket with my address on the back.) I told her to pawn them. She looked horrified – "I wouldn't do that," she said. She'd tried to, of course – I got her to admit it eventually. But her usual broker had been arrested that morning for usury and she was too scared to try another.'

'Gladys...'

'She's dying, did you know? She has a tumour on the back of her neck. Perhaps you didn't notice. Perhaps you had other things on your mind.

'I gave her some money to see a doctor. I almost sent for one there and then. She had walked from Warren Street. It isn't far, from there to St John's Wood; not a long walk for a healthy person. But it took her four hours.'

With that, she raised her hand, drew it back and slapped me hard across the side of my face.

We sat in silence after that, hardly daring to look at each other.

Finally, she said: 'We all want to be better than

we are. But we do not all strive and agonise to be better than we are. We must, though, for that is the true meaning of civilisation.' She looked at me piercingly. 'There must be no secrets between us. So I will open my heart to you and tell you everything.'

I put my arms around her and her head fell against my chest with a terrible sob of pain.

'Do you remember, when I wrote to you and told you that I had gone to the Mafeking celebrations? I regretted saying it as soon as I posted the letter. For while it was true that I did go, it was not celebration I had in mind.

'You should know that for some time now I have been a member of a radical society campaigning for women's suffrage – radical in the sense that we favour direct action. When we try to promote our ideas through meetings and ordinary discourse we are ignored, hence our motto: "Deeds, not words."

'I realise I have told you nothing of my acting life and you were too polite to ask. Perhaps you were embarrassed. All kinds of stories are told, I know, about dressing-room friendships; young girls cooped up in a state of inaction and excitement. I saw something of that. But it did not influence or excite me as much as the women I met on the edge of that theatrical circle – older, wiser women who had really lived and had found the confidence to speak freely and serenely about topics I realised I had been trained to avoid.

'I went to their houses and found the atmosphere extraordinarily congenial. I speak as someone who enjoyed great freedoms growing up despite my father's desire that I should live at home as his assistant rather than earn an independent income. (Latch-key privileges can give a false impression of liberality.)

'One woman in particular made an impression. Anna, she was called. You have heard of Mrs Pankhurst?'

'Of course,' I said.

'Anna had known her when the Pankhursts lived in Russell Square, before they moved back to Manchester seven or eight years ago. She had attended the early meetings of the Women's Franchise League. She had all sorts of ideas, brave ideas. She used to say that women had no economic freedom because they had no political freedom. That only in teaching and the arts were women permitted to thrive. Everywhere else they were barred by prejudice.'

'I don't know about "everywhere".'

'No? How many women lawyers have you come across? Or doctors?'

I said, 'You were talking about the Mafeking celebrations.'

'They were absurd,' said Gladys. 'Really, I wonder what you would have thought, had you been here. Schools were closed. Train drivers blew their whistles for the entire duration of their journeys. All through the Friday night until daybreak the streets were full of shouting, drunken people waving flags and banners. Some rode on the roofs of hansom cabs. Everywhere there were "observances". Restaurants serving "Mafeking menus", theatres and music-halls improvising "Mafeking Day" shows. At the Hippodrome they were handing out pictures of Colonel Baden-Powell as souvenirs.

'Now, I understand that we are at war. I understand that the relief of Mafeking was an important event. But really, the celebrations were disproportionate. No, worse than that: grotesque.

'There is a word the press likes to use to describe suffragist demonstrations: "hysterical". Reporting one, *The Times* noted that some of the "rioters" (though we were no more rioting than flying) were "quite young girls, who must have been the victims of hysteria rather than of deep conviction". *The Times* disapproves of hysteria. But of course in that paper's view the Mafeking celebrations were not hysterical, they were "exhibitions of reckless good temper"!

'You are wondering where this is all going. Patience, my love. It is not a long story.

'At around 11 o'clock on Friday night I went with some other suffragists to the West End. We were disguised as nurses, but took with us posters and pamphlets.

'What did we do? Very little. We put up our posters and painted "Votes For Women" on walls and benches. We damaged a pillar box. Maybe, in our excitement, we broke a window or a street lamp.

'It makes me laugh, comparing the innocuous things we did that night to the actions we were debating in meetings: cutting telephone and telegraph cables; sending envelopes filled with pepper and snuff to Cabinet Ministers. All this will come to pass, I promise you.

'Anyway – we were daubing a wall when a policeman saw us. He blew his whistle and a couple of his colleagues came running. They chased us along the Strand.' Gladys smiled broadly at the memory. 'It was the most thrilling, soul-stirring feeling, losing ourselves among the crowd of revellers on Waterloo Bridge. One woman mistook me for an actual nurse. She asked me to look at her husband, who had collapsed. "Please," she said, "I beg you. He is dying." Well, anyone could see that he was not dying, just drunk. But I crouched beside him and made a show of assessing his condition. As I did so the policemen ran past me. It was a lucky escape.'

'It was foolhardy,' I said, not smiling. 'What happened to your patient?'

'He vomited. Then he got up and announced that he felt much better, thank you very much. The woman hugged me.'

Gladys looked at me. 'You disapprove, I know. You worry about my safety – and, I think, about your own reputation. But the fight for equality is not one I can readily give up or leave to others. If you want me as a wife then you must accept that.'

When she had finished Gladys went over and opened the window. She had brought me some tea, and some bread and butter. As I ate it she sat with me, not saying anything.

Eventually, she asked me if I wanted to read Doyle's letter. I said that I did not.

I lay there, staring out at the unfurnished room, enjoying the warmth of the sun as it poured through the window and the texture of the soft sheets against my body.

Occasionally this idyll was disrupted by a curious noise – a sort of low moan, indescribably sad. It filled the whole air, and yet it was impossible to say whence it came.

I said to Gladys, 'What on earth is that? It's the weirdest, strangest thing that ever I heard in my life.'

She looked up, frowning. 'It might be a bittern,' she said. 'Did you ever hear a bittern booming?'

John O'Connell

Appendix I: Obituary, published in *Daily Express* on Saturday, January 26th, 1907

The announcement of the death of Mr Bertram Fletcher Robinson at the age of 37 will be received with general regret far beyond the circle of his relatives and more immediate friends. He passed away on Monday January 21st 1907 at 44 Eaton Terrace, Belgravia, London, after a short illness, believed to be typhoid fever. He was buried on Thursday at St Andrews' Church, the parish church at Ipplepen, Devon, where he spent his boyhood. A memorial service was also held at St Clement Danes Church, The Strand, London.

The esteem and regard in which he personally was held have been marked by the following eulogy, written by his friend Jessie Pope and published here for the first time:

'Good Bye, kind heart; our benisons preceding,
Shall shield your passing to the other side.
The praise of your friends shall do your
                              pleading
In love and gratitude and tender pride.
To you gay humorist and polished writer,
We will not speak of tears or startled pain.
You made our London merrier and brighter,
God bless you, then, until we meet again!'

Baskerville

Mr Robinson was for several years the Managing Editor of this newspaper. In 1905 he was appointed Editor of *Vanity Fair* and was at the time of his death Editor of the weekly periodical *The World – A Journal for Men and Women*.

Mr Robinson studied at Jesus College, Cambridge where he showed himself to be an able rower and won a rugby 'blue'. He subsequently qualified as a barrister-at-law but never practised, choosing instead to write on rugby for the Isthmian Library series of sporting books – a series he would go on to edit. He had political ambitions and in November 1903 narrowly missed being selected as Liberal Parliamentary Candidate for the Ashburton Division of Devonshire.

His light-hearted stories featuring the detective Addington Peace won many admirers and were collected in a book, 'The Chronicles of Addington Peace', in 1905. But Mr Robinson will be best remembered for his friendship with Sir Arthur Conan Doyle – out of which arose the Sherlock Holmes story 'The Hound of the Baskervilles' – and for the controversy sparked by remarks in the American *Bookseller* magazine over whose contribution was the more significant. [See Appendix III – Ed.]

He is survived by his wife, Gladys, whom he married on June 3rd, 1902, at St Barnabas Church, Kensington, London.

Appendix II: Dedications, etc.

This story owes its inception to my friend, Mr Fletcher Robinson, who has helped me both in the general plot and in the local details – A.C.D.

> **(Note accompanying the first instalment of 'The Hound of the Baskervilles' in the Strand Magazine)**

MY DEAR ROBINSON:
It was to your account of a West-Country legend that this tale owes its inception. For this and for your help in the detail all thanks.
Yours most truly, A. CONAN DOYLE

> **(Dedication from first book version of 'The Hound of the Baskervilles', published by George Newnes in 1902)**

'The Hound of the Baskervilles' arose from a remark by that fine fellow whose premature death was a loss to the world, Fletcher Robinson, that there was a spectral dog near his house on Dartmoor. That remark was the inception of the book, but I should add that the plot and every word of the actual narrative was my own.

> **(From Arthur Conan Doyle's preface to 'The Complete Sherlock Holmes', 1929)**

Appendix III: *Bookseller* controversy

The New Sherlock Holmes Story
Every one who read the opening chapter of the re-
suscitation of Sherlock Holmes in the September
number of the *Strand Magazine* must have come to
the conclusion that Dr Doyle's share in the collaboration was a very small one. 'The Hound of the
Baskervilles' opens very dramatically and promises
to be a very good tale. But the Sherlock Holmes to
whom we are introduced is a totally different per-
sonage from the Sherlock Holmes of 'A Study in
Scarlet', 'The Sign of the Four', 'The Adventures'
and 'The Memoirs'... We have very little hesitation
in expressing our conviction that the story is almost
entirely Mr Robinson's and that Dr Doyle's only
important contribution is the permission to use the
character of Sherlock Holmes.

**(From US edition of *Bookseller* magazine,
October 1901)**

John O'Connell

Appendix IV: Letter from Sir Arthur Conan Doyle to Gladys Robinson

Windlesham,
Crowborough,
Sussex

October 2nd, 1912

My dear Mrs Robinson,

I have been meaning to write this letter for many years. I know you were upset by my failure to attend Bertram's funeral. I can only reiterate what I said at the time − that my work on the Edalji case was all-consuming and I did not have the time to travel down to Ipplepen. I know how that sounds − unfeeling, dismissive. But I am certain your husband would, as a journalist, have understood the zeal that overtakes a man when he is in pursuit of justice and finally has it in his sights.

There are two points I wish to communicate beyond my best wishes and sincere hope that you have found happiness in your new life. The first is that I am more certain than ever of a link between Bertram's death and his investigations − thwarted, as it turns out − into the 'cursed' case of the mummified body of Amon-Ra. I warned Bertram against pursuing this very dark matter, but he would not listen and so his death occurred. I know the immediate cause was given as typhoid fever, but that is the way the Egyptian "elementals" guarding the mummy would work.

The second point is that I recently completed a new book, 'The Lost World'. It has been running in the *Strand* since April so it is possible you have noticed it or even been following it. But you will not have a copy of the book as they are not in the shops until later in the month – so I am enclosing one.

You will note that its hero, Edward E Malone, is a journalist and sportsman who grew up in the West Country; also that he loves a woman called Gladys. At first this Gladys rejects Malone's proposal of marriage because she does not think him a man 'who could do, who could act, who could look Death in the face and have no fear of him, a man of great deeds and strange experiences'.

The kind of man she wishes to love is, she says, a man who makes his own chances. We both know that Bertram was such a man, and that he loved you with all his heart. What is more, I know (though I do not expect you to believe me) that he continues to love you in the ethereal realm that is his current home.

Your friend,
Arthur Conan Doyle

Afterword

The Baskerville Legacy is based on real events. Some of it is speculative in the standard 'biofic' sense that it imagines details, outcomes and conversations which history omitted to record. Just as much, however, is made up for fun: I have always liked books that deliberately straddle or blur the line between fact and fiction.

Not everyone shares this taste, I realise. But had my aim been simply to chronicle 'what actually happened', I would quickly have come unstuck. Documentary evidence of Doyle and Robinson's Dartmoor adventure is thin on the ground and, where it does exist, light on detail.

As far as I know, Robinson never wrote about his holidays with Doyle. An account of walking with Doyle to Grimspound commonly attributed to Robinson – I paraphrase it in one of the diary sections – is in fact from a 1906 *New York Tribune* profile of Doyle by the American journalist Henry Jackson Wells Dam. Whether Dam based the quotations from Robinson on written comments or interviewed him in person – transatlantic phone calls being 20 years away at this point – will never be known.

Doyle did write to his mother from Princetown on June 1st 1901:

Dearest of Mams,

Here I am in the highest town in England. Robinson and I are exploring the moor together over our Sherlock Holmes book. I think it will work splendidly – indeed I have already done nearly half of it. Holmes is at his very best, and it is a highly dramatic idea which I owe to Robinson.

We did 14 miles over the Moor today and we are now pleasantly weary. It is a great place, very sad & wild, dotted with the dwellings of prehistoric man... In those old days there was evidently a population of very many thousands here & now you may walk all day and never see one human being.

This doesn't give much away, though the unwitting shift from '*our* Sherlock Holmes book' to '*I* have already done nearly half of it' is a small joy.

Towards the end of his life, prompted by a Hammer Films publicity team keen to promote the 1959 Peter Cushing/Christopher Lee adaptation of *The Hound of the Baskervilles*, coachman Harry Baskerville came forward with his recollections:

Mr Doyle stayed for eight days and nights. I had to drive him and Bertie about the moors. And I used to watch them in the billiards room in the old house. Sometimes they stayed long into the night, writing and talking together.

Baskerville fed the controversy over the *Hound*'s authorship (which, as Appendix III illustrates, had been bubbling away since 1902) by claiming to have witnessed Robinson writing key sections of the story at Ipplepen, notably the 1742 manuscript outlining the curse of the Baskervilles. He also claimed that both Doyle and Robinson had thanked him for allowing them to use his name.

But Doyle's son Adrian, then literary executor of his father's Estate, refuted this, and in an angry letter to Hammer's publicity supervisor Dennis Thornton wrote:

> *Fletcher Robinson played no part whatever in the writing of the* Hound. *He refused my Father's offer to collaborate and retired at an early stage of the process (*vide *letters, Conan Doyle biographical archives).*

This has the aura of authority based on certain knowledge. But if correspondence between the two men exists, it has never been made public. Certainly, no letters on the subject found their way into *Arthur Conan Doyle: A Life in Letters*, edited by Jon Lellenberg, Daniel Stashower and Charles Foley and published by Harper Press in 2007.

Two eminent Holmes experts, Brian W Pugh and Paul R Spiring, defend Adrian Conan Doyle's assertion insofar as they believe Robinson withdrew from 'full collaboration' on account of his enormous workload. They point out that he had 'some 14 items published in the *Daily Express* and *Pearson's Magazine* during the 16-week period when Doyle was writing…*The Hound of the Baskervilles*. Furthermore, he was commissioned to write 25,000 words of "descriptive letterpress" for a book entitled *Sporting Pictures* that was subsequently published by Cassell & Company in 1902.'

Pugh and Spiring believe Doyle and Robinson remained close friends until the latter's death from typhoid – contracted after drinking tap water from a sink in his Paris hotel room – in 1907. The pair continued to play golf together and were inducted in 1904 into an exclusive criminological society known simply as Our Society alongside their friend, the writer of boys' adventure stories Max Pemberton. Pemberton's theory of fiction, as outlined in an interview with Meredith Starr for her book *The Future of the Novel* (Heath Cranton, 1921), I cheekily put into Doyle's mouth in Chapter 5.

Andrew Lycett, in his 2007 biography *Conan Doyle: The Man Who Invented Sherlock Holmes* (Weidenfeld & Nicolson, 2007), suggests Robinson was actually paid handsomely for his work as plot consultant, taking a third of the unprecedented £100-per-thousand-words fee which Doyle negotiated for himself: 'Arthur's bank account book does indeed show him paying Robinson over £500 in the latter half of 1901, but subsequent payments were more sporadic.' The letter from Doyle to Herbert Greenhough Smith quoted in Chapter 7 is genuine, and Doyle did subsequently write another letter, which I do not quote, revealing his plans to resurrect Holmes and asking for his fee to be adjusted accordingly.

Gladys I have more or less invented as I was able to find out little about her beyond her painter father and an unattributed remark that she was a 'self-proclaimed actress' – a funny thing to proclaim in 1901 if, as seems to be the case here, there was some doubt about the matter, for the word 'actress' was still synonymous in some quarters with 'prostitute'. I based her on flinty Gladys Hungerton in *The Lost World* with a dash of the eponymous heroine of HG Wells' *Ann Veronica* (Fisher Unwin, 1909). Her little speech about the rituals of African women is taken from Sir James George Fraser's pioneering anthropological work *The Golden Bough: A Study in Magic and Religion* (Macmillan, 1890), which I like to imagine she had just read.

Yes, I know the term 'suffragette' wasn't coined until 1906; also that the kind of demonstrations I have Gladys participating in did not occur until later in the decade when suffrage movements became more radicalised. But it felt right to have her protesting against the Mafeking celebrations in this way. Incidentally, the riot Gladys describes in the Crystal Palace tearoom is a nod to a scene in George Gissing's bleakly brilliant novel *The Nether World* (Elder & Co, 1889). I liked the idea of her being there to witness it.

Arthur Coddling is an invention, but Madame D'Esperance aka Elizabeth Hope did exist and her 'spirit guide' Yolande really was assaulted midséance. Whether Hope knew Doyle is hard to say. It's possible: he was a committed researcher into the paranormal and had been a member of the Society for Psychical Research since November 1893.

Hesketh Hesketh-Pritchard really did go to Patagonia to hunt down the Mylodon for the *Daily Express*. The passage declaimed by Robinson is from *Through the Heart of Patagonia* (Heinemann, 1902), his subsequent account of the trip. As well as a writer, adventurer and professional cricketer, Hesketh-Pritchard was an expert sniper who would be credited with dramatically improving the sorry quality of British marksmanship on the Western Front.

The Sexton of St Andrew's church in Ipplepen did have a daughter called Alice and she did die young. Details of the ledger in which parish burials were recorded can be found in Arthur French's pamphlet *Ipplepen* (Obelisk Publications, 2003).

Of the many liberties I have taken, the most

egregious to experts in the field of Doyle studies will be my transformation of Bertram Fletcher Robinson from the solid, uncomplicated fellow I suspect he was into an agonised, drug-addicted, prostitute-visiting egotist. I can only apologise and plead authorial necessity (and my own addiction to Victorian sensation novels). Anyone wanting to find out more about the real historical Bertram Fletcher Robinson should visit the excellent website run by Paul R Spiring at www.bfronline.biz.

Robinson had some success with his Addington Peace stories, most of which were published in *The Lady's Home Magazine* between August 1904 and January 1905 and collected as *The Chronicles of Addington Peace* (Harper & Brother, 1905). I have scattered little phrases and fragments from the stories throughout *The Baskerville Legacy*. In particular, the sections of *The Wolf of the Baskervilles* that Robinson imagines Doyle reading are modified quotations from 'The Terror in the Snow'. The other Peace story I refer to, 'The Tragedy of Thomas Hearne', could well have been started in Princetown and is clearly cut from the same cloth as *The Hound of the Baskervilles*, escaped convict and all.

Some of Doyle's dialogue is paraphrased from letters and other writings. The quotation from Sir John Robinson's *Fifty Years of Fleet Street* (Macmillan, 1904) is genuine.

The prefatory letter from Robinson to his solicitor is imagined. In the appendices, Robinson's obituary (Appendix I) is made up, though Jessie Pope's eulogy is genuine. Appendix II is all genuine, as is Appendix III. Appendix IV is imagined.

~

I first encountered the story of Doyle and Robinson in 1996 in Christopher Frayling's book *Nightmare: The Birth of Horror* (BBC Books, 1996), the tie-in to an inspired and entertaining TV series which really ought to be repeated on BBC4 at some point. Frayling reworked and expanded this chapter into an introduction to the most recent (2004) Penguin Classics edition of *The Hound of the Baskervilles*.

In addition to the books and website mentioned above I made use of the following titles while researching this novel: *On the Trail of Arthur Conan Doyle: An Illustrated Devon Tour* by Brian W Pugh and Paul R Spiring (Book Guild, 2008); *Bertram Fletcher Robinson: A Footnote to "The Hound of the Baskervilles"* by Brian W Pugh and Paul R Spiring (MX Publishing, 2008); *The Hound of the Baskervilles: Hunting the Dartmoor Legend* by Philip Weller (Devon Books, 2001); *Dartmoor and its Surroundings* by Beatrix Cresswell (Beechings, 1899); *A Book of Dartmoor* by Sabine Baring-Gould (Methuen, 1900); *The*

Intellectuals and the Masses by John Carey (Faber, 1992); *Faces of the Living Dead* by Martyn Jolly (British Library, 2006); *Shadow Land* by Elizabeth D'Esperance (Redway, 1897); *The Victorian Internet* by Tom Standage (Weidenfeld & Nicolson, 1998); *Fifty Years on the Diamond Fields, 1870-1920* by RJL Sabatini (Kimblerley Africana Library, 2007); *Memories and Adventures* by Arthur Conan Doyle (Hodder & Stoughton, 1924); *The Life of Sir Arthur Conan Doyle* by John Dickson Carr (John Murray, 1949).

Thank you to everyone at Short Books; Antony Topping at Greene & Heaton; Katherine Stroud; and early readers Cathy Newman, Alex O'Connell, Antonia Hodgson and Alice Fisher for helpful comments.

John O'Connell worked for several years at the
London listings magazine *Time Out*, where he was
Books Editor. He now writes, mostly about books,
for *The Times*, *The Guardian*, *New Statesman* and
The National. He is the author of *I Told You I Was Ill:
Adventures in Hypochondria* (Short Books, 2005)
and *The Midlife Manual* (Short Books, 2010). He is
37 and lives in south London with his wife and
two children.